Murder,
so Sweet

A Novel By

DAVE VIZARD

Also by Dave Vizard

Murder, Key West Style
A Place for Murder
A Formula for Murder
A Grand Murder
Murder in the Wind

Copyright ©2023 Dave Vizard
All rights reserved

About this novel

This is a work of fiction. Names, characters, places, and incidents are either the product of the author's imagination or used fictitiously. Any resemblance to actual persons, living or dead, business establishments, events, or locales is entirely coincidental.

Credits

Edited by: Christina M. Frey, J.D., Christina@pagetwoediting.com
Final edit and proof reading: Janis Stein, steinexpressions.com
Cover design: Alan Garcia, alan@we-ru.com
Design and formatting: Duane Wurst, duane0w@gmail.com

ISBN: 979-8--218-12800-5

Printed in the United State of America

Acknowledgements:

Murder, so Sweet came to life with the help of many hands. In addition to the very talented and gifted folks listed under Credits on the previous page, I have to give a shout out to many friends in the legal community who helped with navigation through their waters. Of course, it always helps a murder mystery writer to have a lawyer as an editor and a son who is active and practicing in Michigan. Many thanks to son, Mickey, a defense attorney in Genesee County, who acted as a firm but flexible guardrail through the court system associated with this story. One other note of special thanks. Alan Garcia, who designed the cover for this novel, is a former co-worker from my days at The Bay City Times. It was absolutely delightful for me to collaborate with him on a project again. It brought back many fond memories of all the great work that we accomplished at The Times. Thanks Alan. I'm so glad I was able to arm twist, cajole, wheedle, and sweet-talk you into taking on this project. And, as always, we made deadline with style.

Dedication

This story is for my brothers, Frank and Mike, who have always been great storytellers in their own right. I learned much from them over the years, and they seldom took me off the straight and narrow. But, when they did, we had a hell of lot of fun! Thanks guys. Love you much.

Frank, Dave, and Mike - the Vizard brothers.

Chapter 1
Monday Morning
Bay City Blade **Newsroom**

Nick Steele twirled the wedding band on his left ring finger as he scrolled through a news story in the *Bay City Blade* newsroom. It was his latest project, a piece looking at the disconnect between Bay City and its lost daughter, Madonna, the wildly successful pop star.

Since her heyday, the *Blade* had published more than a dozen articles about Madonna, her Bay City roots, and her family members who still called the mid-Michigan city their hometown. The articles focused on local efforts to bring Madonna back to Bay City for the presentation of a key to the city and a big community group hug. Sadly, a series of miscommunications and bungled overtures made the city appear as though it were begging her on bended knee to come home while the pop star coolly ignored their pleas.

Nick's story was about the growing movement among community leaders who wanted to work with the singer to develop the Madonna Academy of Music and Theatre, which would, of course, be headquartered in Bay City.

Appealing to her flair for creativity and innovation might be just the ticket to pull her back home, some thought. Nick—and many others—believed it was a long shot. But why not throw a Hail Mary with a hope and prayer to land Madonna?

Nick's work on the story had sparked newsroom controversy. Some reporters and editors asked out loud why the hotshot reporter, who had covered murders, kidnappings, and other high-profile crimes, had now scored a premium feature assignment. It stank of favoritism, people said. Nick and his allies chalked that up to petty jealousies. Still, he was glad the piece was almost finished.

As he polished the story, he fiddled with the ring he'd worn happily since marrying Tanya, his longtime love, four months earlier in Key West. Feeling the band was comforting, and he caught himself doing it routinely.

Nick was about to store and close the story, when one of the reporters from the sports department yelled across the newsroom, "Hey, Nick, got a call for you. Pick up line four."

"Can you take a message for me?" Nick shouted back, his voice rising above the usual newsroom din.

"I'm not your secretary, Nick. Guy says it's important. Says his name is Booger."

Nick's eyes lit up. It was Deputy J.R. Ratchett from the Huron County Sheriff's Office. If Boog was calling, it must be important. The reporter hit line four. "Hey, deputy. Always good to hear from you. What's happening?" The two had become friendly over the years after working together on important stories from the Thumb.

"Nick, you ol' three-legged coyote, how you doin'? Ain't talked to you since you got hitched to that purdy little filly, Tanya," Booger said. "You two still talking to each other now that you tied the knot?"

The reporter laughed. Chatting with Deputy Ratchett was a treat, and Nick almost always ended up with a good news tip. He was eager to hear what was on the lawman's mind this time. "We're doing good," Nick said. "I'll tell her you asked. You calling from Bad Axe? Is the town burning down, or what?"

The line went quiet, which meant the deputy had disturbing news—the kind no one liked delivering.

Booger cleared his throat, beginning his tale in a solemn voice. "Nick, it's bad, real bad. Never seen anything like it, and I'll bet you ain't either."

That made Nick sit up straight in his chair. He covered his right ear with his hand, hoping to block out the boisterous newsroom chatter.

Finally, Booger spit it out. "Body tissue. We got body tissue in a farm field. It's mixed with natural fertilizer and spread out in a huge field."

"Natural fertilizer?"

"Cow shit." As Ratchett explained it, the farm owner had begun spring tilling and turned up a shocking surprise. Before the first furrow was complete, it was swarmed by seagulls, which often descended on plowed fields to feed on freshly exposed worms and insects. But it soon became apparent the flying scavengers, now numbering in the hundreds, were feasting on something else. They took turns dive-bombing the open space, picking body tissue out of the soil. Upon closer review, J.R. said, the farmer had found a piece of finger, which almost hit him when it fell from the clutches of a bird. Also found: human hair and part of what looked like an ear.

The information hit Nick like a John Deere diesel. Body parts in the Thumb, the area of Michigan where Nick had grown up. The Thumb had always been peaceful, family-oriented farm country—not a graveyard. He asked the deputy who knew about the tissue discovery.

"Just us county mounties so far, but that won't last," Booger said. "State police are sending a mobile forensics team and some troopers to help protect the crime scene. We'll have lots of gawkers out here too, no doubt. I called you because I knew you'd do us right with the story. No sensationalism. This is wild enough as it is, and the media will be circling it like them seagulls out there in the field."

Boog was right. "Where do I find you? I'm working on a feature about Madonna, but it can wait."

"Madonna? Why are you writin' about that burned-out old hag? Overdose? Alcoholic coma? Did AIDS get her?"

Whoa! Nick tried to cool down Boog. Just a new story about the Bay City native, he said. He asked again where to find the deputy—or the farm field.

Ratchett said the body tissue was in a field off highway M-142, right outside Pigeon and not far from Laker High School. Follow the seagulls, he said, they'd be flying in from Lake Huron and they'd lead him to the scene of the crime.

"And one more thing, Nick," the deputy said, falling back into his measured, somber tone. "Could be more than one body out there. It's a big-ass field."

Chapter 2
Monday, early afternoon
Near Laker High School, Pigeon

Indeed, it was a big-ass field. Nick parked his gold Firebird on the side of M-142 and walked a quarter mile down a gravel road toward the cloud of white birds circling frantically over the field.

Shotgun blasts boomed into the sky several minutes apart. Deputies were firing buckshot, hoping to keep the seagulls from making off with the evidence.

The birds, squawking and feverishly dive-bombing despite the blasts, seemed to be hanging closer to the road. Nick watched the frenzy against the deep blue sky and the quickening pace of law enforcement on the ground below them.

Deputies and troopers dressed in light-green coveralls, plastic gloves, goggles, and face masks marched down the field, using small hand rakes to sift through the soil and pluck out anything that looked like human tissue.

It was a horrible task on a cool spring day, when farmers would normally be planting crops. Instead the area was blocked off from all directions while officers crept down the length of the field. The smell of manure was pungent and, at times, overpowering. Nick watched one searcher pause to remove their mask and gag or vomit before returning to work.

Deputy Ratchett stood in the road, his county cruiser parked crossways to block traffic and keep folks away from the crime scene. He recognized Nick and waved him forward.

"Now, remember, you did not get this news tip from me. Sheriff would skin me alive if he knew I was talking to you," J.R. said. He swept his left arm in the direction of the field. "The first furrow sticks close to the tree line along the ditch. Your girl has the perfect view."

"Huh? My girl?" Nick strained to see whom the deputy was talking about.

"No, up there," J.R. said, pointing his chin upward. "She's up in that big-ass oak tree, and she sure looks young to me. You confident she's out of high school?"

Nick scanned the tree line and spotted Anne Simmons, a *Blade* photographer and videographer, strapped to a tree limb about halfway up an eighty-foot oak. Anne had tied herself to a limb that hung far out over the field. With her right leg wrapped around the branch, and a yellow strap, fashioned into a harness, tethering her to it, she worked an assortment of cameras and recording devices dangling from her neck.

Anne was young, but she was fearless. She took big chances to get the unforgettable image, and she usually came away successful.

"Holy shit, Anne, be careful up there," Nick yelled, cupping his hands around his mouth. He wasn't sure she could hear him, but he was confident she had found a terrific vantage point. "Where did you get that yellow strap?"

Anne did not respond immediately—she was busy recording a piece of history. "Hey, Nick. Don't worry, it's tough nylon. It's a tow rope I keep in my trunk in case Betsy, my piece-of-crap Toyota, poops out."

The reporter was glad he had stopped to update his managing editor on his way out of the newsroom. Drayton Clapper had understood this was an important story. The newsroom chief had sent Anne, rerouting her from a news conference in Essexville, to the Thumb. He'd also sent Dave Balz, a veteran reporter and Nick's best friend, to the crime scene. Dave was already at the far end of the field, interviewing the farmer tilling the field and Roderick Bennett, the landowner.

"Anybody had a chance to examine the tilled-up body parts?" Nick asked, scribbling notes as quickly as his pen would move. He looked at J.R.'s face, hoping to see a reaction. Nothing but Booger's unfazed mug. "Are the pieces random, or do they have a common shape and size?" he asked.

The deputy said it was too early to tell much about the tissue. "But right now those bagging the parts say this ain't *Fargo*—if that's what you're asking."

Nick nodded. If a wood or brush chipper wasn't used, then what had done the grinding? His mind raced.

"I'm going to have to get ugly with you for a few minutes, Nick," the deputy said, motioning down the gravel road toward a cloud of dust. It was the county sheriff, a control freak who wanted all event publicity to make him look like the toughest lawman since Wyatt Earp. "Don't take this personal. Gotta make it sound like I'm a real prick with the media."

Sheriff Eric Donaldson roared toward them, lights flashing and siren screaming, all four wheels churning. His Chevy SUV slid sideways, spraying gravel across Booger's cruiser like it had been shot up by a pellet gun.

But the sheriff did not admonish J.R.; he wanted to give his deputy a heads-up. Word about the discovery of body tissue had spread fast. Relatives of locals reported missing during the last few months were hounding the sheriff. In the Thumb, families were close-knit. Many people shared each other's pain, grief, and joy, and helped their neighbors through crises.

"Boog, we gotta put out a statement to the media," Donaldson said, his breathing fast and ragged like he had run the fourteen miles from Bad Axe to Pigeon. "The undersheriff is surveying all the counties around us to see how many missing persons they have, but some of these mothers ain't waitin' around."

"We're in luck, chief. This here is Nick Steele from the *Bay City Blade*," J.R. said. "Give him your statement. He can spread the word."

"Who's the monkey in the tree?"

"Ah, that's Anne. She works with Nick. And over across the field talking with the landowner is Dave. That's all the media here so far." The deputy looked up the gravel road toward the main highway. A fire engine from nearby Elkton had been called in to block the side road to keep the gawkers, ghouls, and grievers from getting too close to the crime scene.

It wasn't working. Already a giant wooden cross had been erected in the field across from the crime scene, with folks from all walks of life assembling around the cross. They carried glass candles, flowers, and mementos from their missing loved ones.

Sister S., a nun who worked with Catholic Family Services, stood at the center of the growing crowd and prayed loudly: "Our Father, who art in heaven, hallowed be thy name …" Slowly, townsfolk dropped to their knees in the muddy field to recite the Lord's Prayer and the others that followed.

The sheriff directed J.R. to go speak to the folks surrounding the cross. He hoped his deputy, who knew most by their first names, could calm their fears. "Boog, they're starting to freak out because of what they don't know. See if you can help them. I'll talk to Nick here and the landowner. We need to find out who had access to this field to dump the tissue."

The deputy nodded and jumped in his cruiser. As he inched toward the intersection, he spotted Sarah Robbins, who was running as fast as her short, stubby legs could carry her, straight at Boog's cruiser. The deputy knew exactly what was on her mind.

"Hey, Boog," she shouted. She'd stopped in the center of the road, waving her arms as if the deputy could not see her. "Is Elroy out there in that field? Is he all cut up in bits and pieces? He hasn't been home in three days."

The deputy could not say for certain it wasn't Elroy in the field, but he had a pretty good idea the tissue was not from Sarah's husband of forty-six years. He stepped out of his vehicle and approached the distraught woman.

"Sarah, we are still sorting things out—still investigating. But if I was a bettin' man, I'd put my money on Elroy being off on another bender. My guess is, he'll show up when he runs out of beer money."

The woman collapsed in the deputy's arms, sobbing. "You're most likely right, but every time he takes off, I wonder if he's coming back. When I heard about body parts in the field this morning, I had this awful feeling it was Elroy."

As Ratchett soon found out, Sarah and her feelings were not alone. Among those gathered around the cross were the spouses of dementia patients who'd wandered off after becoming confused and disoriented. Moms of runaway teens comforted each other, wept, and prayed.

As he tried to reassure the growing crowd, the deputy caught his first glimpse of a media mob rolling down M-142: television news trucks with giant satellite dishes strapped to their roofs.

Boog sighed and mumbled to himself, "This is going to get ugly."

Chapter 3
Monday evening
St. Clementine's Catholic Church

Like a finely tuned timepiece, Andrea Pilinski chugged into the front entrance of St. Clementine's at precisely seven in the evening. The eighty-two-year-old South End widow never missed her opportunity for Monday night confession, though the sacrament was offered on Wednesdays and Fridays as well. Monday night confessions were a long-honored tradition at St. Clementine's. They harkened back to the sawmill era of Bay City, when hard-partying men confessed their sinful deeds after a drunken weekend, prayed for forgiveness, and vowed to never do it again—or at least until the next Friday night came along.

These days, however, only a handful of parishioners found their way to the church on the first workday of the week. Tonight was no different. A few heads bobbed up and down among those kneeling in prayer and reflection.

Andrea took a deep breath and removed black earmuffs from her mop of short silver-blond curls. She nodded in the direction of the Andersons, also Monday night regulars.

The line outside the confessional was short. Mrs. Anderson, crowding eighty, stood along the wall, her scarved head bowed. Mr. Anderson, slender and bent over by a spine shaped like a question mark from years on an assembly line, lit candles near the altar.

Andrea knelt in an empty pew near the back of the church, praying quietly in the shadows.

When a younger woman entered, genuflected, and blessed herself, Andrea, deep in reflection, hardly noticed. The strange woman paused, studying the two older people waiting to tell Father Bob their

Murder, so Sweet 15

sins. She took a seat in a pew near the corner of the church, where three telephone booth–sized closets comprised the confessional.

The light went on over the middle closet, meaning Father Bob was ready to hear confessions. Scarf Lady and Question Mark Man shuffled toward the confessionals, each one entering an empty closet. All three lights above the confessionals flickered in the dim glow.

About ten minutes passed before Scarf Lady stepped out of the confessional, her head still bowed and her hands clasped under her chin. Slowly she made her way toward the lit candles. She would wait there for her partner, who was in the midst of a coughing fit in his closet.

Once the wheezing and hacking subsided, low murmuring between the two men resumed. Soon the wooden window slid closed, and Question Mark Man opened the closet door. He squinted across the shadowy church, then joined Scarf Lady kneeling near the candles.

Andrea kept an eye on the couple, paying little attention to the stranger now entering one of the confessionals. The older woman said three more Hail Marys, then strode toward the remaining open confessional. As she passed the priest's perch between the two, she heard his voice rise from a whisper, telling the confessor that remorse and repentance were key elements of confession.

Andrea tried to block out the conversation between Father Bob and the stranger. She entered the confessional, pulled the door shut until it clicked, and knelt and completed a final search of her soul before spilling the worst of it to her parish priest.

The discussion in the next confessional was growing heated. The younger woman was speaking, her voice no longer a whisper. Andrea looked up. She wondered if she should cover her ears with her hands or her black muffs.

"I'm responsible for a man's death," the stranger declared. "Well, actually, it's two men, but the dirty bastards deserved it!"

Andrea gasped, covering her mouth quickly. Had she heard a confession to murder? She leaned in toward the screen covering the priest's window, turning her "good ear" in the direction of the raised voices.

"My child, my child. Taking the life of another is the most serious sin, and you say you killed two men," Father Bob said in a somber tone. "You can ask for forgiveness, but you must be truly remorseful. Are you remorseful?"

"Hell no, I'm not remorseful," the young woman said, her voice rising with rage. "I'd do it again tomorrow if I had to."

"I'm sorry, but I cannot offer absolution for your sins if you are not remorseful and repentant."

The stranger continued: "Oh, I'm sorry about the lying, card cheating, cursing, and taking the Lord's name in vain. I feel awful about those things, and I will do my best to not repeat them. But the killing of walking, talking vermin? Hell no! I will never be sorry for it."

Andrea thought she heard the door of the stranger's confessional open.

"My child, this is not something you can run away from," the priest said. "Murder will haunt you the rest of your days. Guilt is what brought you here today. Those feelings will not go away on their own. Please, let's talk more."

The confessional door slammed. Andrea pictured the woman dashing through a mostly empty church like she was being chased by wolf hounds.

Father Bob opened his confessional door in time to see the front door close. He returned to his seat and composed himself, clearing his throat and coughing gently into his hand.

Andrea knelt in silence, struggling to collect her thoughts.

After a few moments, the wood panel separating the two slid open. "What's troubling you today, my child?" Father Bob said in an even, measured voice.

The priest's greeting caught Andrea by surprise. How could he be so calm—like nothing had happened? Had she really heard what she thought she had?

Her own list of sins, so puny and pitiful when compared to murder, escaped her. Andrea searched the corners of her mind. What had she planned to confess to Father Bob? She could not remember a single transgression.

Andrea tried to push the shocking words from her mind. In more than seventy years of going to confession regularly, she was dumbstruck by what she'd heard: two men murdered. She started her confession with the basic introduction, then resorted to a short list of her regular sins: "I fibbed to one of my friends twice, I had impure thoughts about a male member of the parish, I missed morning prayers because my alarm clock did not go off, and I did not say grace before lunch with the girls one day this week. Of these sins, I am most remorseful for the fibbing and will do my best to not do it again."

After a short pause, Father Bob said, "Is that it?"

Embarrassed by her lightweight list, she replied in a whisper, "Yes, Father."

Andrea wanted to ask Father Bob about what she'd heard, but felt ashamed for listening to the strange woman's confession. Besides, she reasoned, a priest couldn't discuss what went on in the confessional, so it would be pointless to ask.

Outside St. Clementine's, Natalie O'Brien sat in her red Plymouth van and smoked a Virginia Slims cigarette, cursing herself for going into the church in the first place. She'd broken a pact she'd made with her brother and sister. They had sworn to each other they would never tell anyone about the murders, and now she'd gone and blabbed to a priest.

Worse, she worried her confession had been overheard. She was certain someone had entered the third confessional while she proclaimed that she'd killed two men, had no remorse for the murders, and would do it again. Natalie knew she'd raised her voice while confessing, but was it loud enough for someone else to hear? She lit a second cigarette from the butt of the first and watched until the front door of the church opened.

Question Mark Man emerged with his wife, who removed the scarf from her head and placed it in her handbag. The two helped each other amble across the street. The couple seemed harmless, but Natalie was not so sure about the other person who had been in the church. If she'd overheard the confession, she was a threat to Natalie and her family. The distraught woman pulled on her Virginia Slim so hard, the glow from the burning end lit up the dashboard of her van.

Soon the front door to the church opened again, and Andrea stepped outside into the cool evening air. She looked up into the streetlight and placed her black earmuffs onto the sea of curls. Natalie thought she recognized the woman from one of the Bay City civic organizations she belonged to.

When the woman slid into the driver's seat of a yellow 1975 Cadillac Coupe de Ville, Natalie remembered where she'd seen the car parked—Bay City Noon Optimists. A smile spread across her face, and she relaxed. She vowed to track down the eavesdropper. After hunting two strange men from different cities and killing them, she'd have no difficulty finding a woman with silver-blond curls, black earmuffs, and an ancient yellow Caddy.

Chapter 4
Monday night
Bay City Blade newsroom

Dave Balz paced the floor next to Nick's desk, squeezing a red rubber ball with one hand. He passed it to the other for more aggressive kneading.

"Stop walking, you're driving me crazy," Nick said. He flipped through his notes from the day. "We've got to push this story again tomorrow."

A copy of the final afternoon pressrun was spread out on the desk. Its main headline was in 72-point type: "Murder, so sweet," and the underline—in 30-point type—read "Investigators unearth human remains in Thumb sugar beet field." The article was accompanied by Anne's photos of seagulls swarming the field.

The story detailed what the reporters had learned so far. Dave had interviewed the property owner, Roderick Bennett, who farmed a thousand acres of mostly sugar beets and corn with his wife and two sons. Bennett maintained he had no idea how human tissue had ended up in his field. He said the field was on a regular fertilizer schedule, getting liquid cow manure spread on it twice a year—spring and fall. It would then be plowed under before a new crop was planted. By now, investigators had excavated most of the field, and the tissue appeared limited to a quarter of it. The Huron County Medical Examiner's Office had been on the scene all day. Its initial findings: the human tissue belonged to two middle-aged males, and their bones had been sawed, not chipped or smashed.

Nick wondered if the bodies had gone through a professional processing plant. The Thumb was home to hundreds of deer hunters, many of whom processed and packaged their own kill. It would not be uncommon to find barns or big sheds with slaughterhouse equipment that could be put to work for an entirely different reason.

What Dave did not report in his article was that the Bennetts' neighbors whispered out loud about the family's tendency toward sticky fingers, picking up unattended farm equipment in open fields and selling the expensive tools on the ag black market across the Midwest. The Bennetts' eldest son, Rory, had been caught by the state police while he was loading a tractor on a flatbed. He couldn't produce proof of ownership, and Rory got two years in the slammer for his misdeeds. The family's reputation in the Thumb took a drubbing.

But thievery didn't necessarily make them killers.

Chief Donaldson did not disappoint the readers of the *Blade*, which circulated to fifty thousand readers in thirteen northeast Michigan counties, including the Thumb and Mackinac Island. Though he cited no proof, the chief opined to Nick that the body tissue, mixed with natural fertilizer and spread in a farm field, looked like the work of the mob.

"I think it's a mob hit related to drug trafficking, and they are sending a message," he said. "Instead of sending a dead fish to signify their target is swimming with the fishes in a lake, they spread the remains with manure to suggest their victim is now covered in excrement and feeding worms in the dirt. Who wants to go out like that?"

"Best quote—ever," Nick declared as he reread the passage. Dave challenged him on it: the sheriff, facing reelection and a crowded field of opponents, could not possibly have said something as wild and crazy as that.

"I got it on tape," Nick said, reaching for his recorder. The newsman fumbled with the device before it clicked on and the newsroom filled with the shrill voice of the sheriff and his outlandish theory. But it didn't stop there. The sheriff also speculated that the killings were the work of street gangs from Flint and Saginaw. He suggested gangs might have killed their own members and hoped to discard them undetected in the wide-open fields of the Thumb.

The sheriff's speculations did have a basis in local lore. The Thumb was remote and rural but located less than two hours from metro Detroit, Flint, and Saginaw, which gave those cities fast and easy access to the sticks for unsavory folks keen to hide secrets, embarrassments, or criminal activity.

Legend had it the Thumb was the northern playground for the Purple Gang, notorious for its bootlegging, prostitute peddling, and murderous ways in the 1920s and '30s. It operated primarily from Detroit's East Side.

The sheriff's theories played into the legend, and many Thumb residents would buy into any notion that the human tissue was placed in that farm field by forces outside of their friends, neighbors, and relatives.

Deputy Ratchett had privately offered Nick another theory he said was gaining traction among farmers in the Thumb. The body tissue, they said, could be from human traffickers who regularly smuggled undocumented workers into the area to milk and maintain cows on the area's huge dairy farms.

"You know it from working on the Suzie Alvarez story," Booger said. "Getting rid of bodies if people die in transit or from accidents is a problem for human smugglers. Plowing under the remains alleviates that problem."

As Nick relayed Booger's theory to Dave, his office phone rang—the security guard at the front door. "Hide your beers, the C-Man just entered the building."

The C-Man was Drayton Clapper, managing editor of the *Blade*, who had stopped at the office after a Chamber of Commerce board meeting. The guard rightly believed it was a good idea to alert Nick and Dave because they had both been previously fired for drinking in the newsroom.

The guys stashed their open beers in the trash, then covered the cans with papers from Nick's desk. They busied themselves with make-work as Clapper strolled into the newsroom, carrying a small cardboard box under his right arm.

"Hey, guys, great work today!" The chief sauntered toward their desks, shaking trash cans as he walked. "What's the plan for tomorrow?"

Nick and Dave glanced at each other with alarm. The C-Man was showing unusual interest in the trash containers he encountered along the way—was their boss on to them?

"We're obviously going back to the scene of the crime," Nick said, eyeing the trash can where he and Dave had hidden the damning evidence. The C-Man stopped right beside it, smiling. Nick added, "We expect to learn more on all fronts of the case. Booger, ah, Deputy Ratchett, said sheriff's departments from Huron, Tuscola, and Sanilac Counties were compiling lists of all those who had been reported missing during the last two years."

Plus, the shrine next to the crime scene continued growing, Booger had told Nick. It now looked like Mount Calvary, with three crosses erected amid a multitude of candles, flowers, wreaths, photos, poetry, and other mementos from family members and friends of the missing. Nick and Dave planned to interview each of them and document their losses in case the remains in the field ended up being a loved one. Their stories needed to be told.

Meanwhile, tips were rolling in to the sheriff's department and the *Blade*. Everyone, it seemed, who had a loved one missing wanted to know if they were in that field. Phones were ringing with tips about potential monsters who might have carved up the bodies—from hated ex-husbands to weird loner neighbors.

Clapper had requested a clerk from another department to help handle all the phone calls. He instructed the clerk to document each call. While some calls were the rantings of maniacs, others seemed sincere and wanted to help. And someone out in the general public might have heard or seen something that could lead investigators to the killers.

Still, hard evidence aside from the body tissue itself was tough to come by.

"The big thing we are waiting on is DNA," Nick said, walking away from his desk—and the trash container near it. Identifying the remains would be impossible unless the cops found a match in their databases. "But if these two mystery guys never got arrested or had their DNA collected, we got nothing to compare it to."

The C-Man nodded. Keep working it, he said, and keep the news desk posted. He used his left foot to kick the trash bin next to Nick's desk. Cans clanked as they collided and spilled, filling the newsroom with the distinctive odor of beer.

Sniffing the air, the C-Man declared, "My gosh, that smells an awful lot like Budweiser. But I know you guys would never drink in the newsroom after the last time. You learned your lesson then, didn't you?"

Nick and Dave nodded like a couple of bobbleheads that had had their noggins tapped. They watched Clapper stroll to Dave's desk, where he opened the bottom left drawer and plucked out two cans of unopened Bud. He tossed one can to Dave and the other to Nick. He also tossed the small box he'd carried into the newsroom onto Nick's desk.

"Guard said this box was left for you at the front desk just before closing," the chief said. "And those two Buds are for you to drink at home, which is where I suggest you go."

The C-Man snatched another beer from Dave's desk and stuck it in his pocket. As the editor headed for the door, Nick opened the box, which was wrapped in plain brown paper. His name was printed on the top in black marker.

Clapper stopped in his tracks when he heard the shriek.

"Holy shit! What the hell?" Nick yelled, dropping the box on the floor. The three men stood looking down at the contents, which had plopped out onto the carpet. There before them in full color were the pink tips of two small penises and a folded piece of paper.

All three men popped open their beers and chugged them down greedily, their Adam's apples jumping up and down like bouncing tennis balls. Each belched, almost on cue, the grotesque noise echoing across the empty newsroom. They blinked at the floor, not wanting to believe what their eyes were telling them.

Dave spoke first: "Now, there's something you don't see every day."

Nick reached for the folded paper, but the C-Man blocked his hand. "Let's call the cops in to handle it. Looks like evidence to me."

Chapter 5
Late Monday night
Bay City Blade newsroom

When investigators from the Bay City Police Department invaded the *Blade* newsroom, they confirmed what the journalists' eyes had told them. Two penis tips had indeed fallen out of the box.

Officer Dan Quinn used a set of tweezers to pick up and examine each one. "Ah, what a wee little pecker we've got here," he said, rotating the two-inch tip for closer inspection. "Looks like it's been frozen and recently thawed, judging by the frost mark and the amount of moisture in the box. But we'll send them both off to the lab."

The C-Man kept a close eye on the other officers in the newsroom. He didn't want them rummaging through reporter desks or files. He and the *Blade* attorneys called to the scene made it clear most areas were off limits. For now, though, the police were interested only in the two penises, the box, and the guard at the front desk who'd received the package.

Nick had already interviewed the guard by the time Quinn and his cohorts showed up at the front door of the *Blade* building. But the guard had nothing to report.

"It was right here when I punched in," the man said, poking around his trash can to find the note that had been taped to the box. He pawed past a burger wrapper, used ketchup packets, and a few cold fries to retrieve the note. "Here it is: 'Give to Nick Steele' in black marker. The grease stains are compliment of the fries."

Nick had suggested the guard give it to the police. The reporter was much more interested in the note that had fallen out of the box

25

with the body parts.

Quinn used two sets of tweezers to pick up the paper and unfold it.

The handwritten note, also in black marker, said "Here are a couple of tips. Stop the rapes or the seagulls will continue to feed. This is just the beginning. —Vigilant Vigilantes."

Dave photographed the note. Quinn tucked it into an evidence bag to go with the body parts to the lab for evaluation.

"Damn, have we got a serial killer or killers on our hands?" Nick asked. "Stop the rapes? More gulls feeding? Vigilant Vigilantes?"

Dave became animated, holding his hands up in the air. "I can see the book title for this story right now: *V.V.—The Vagina Vigilantes.*"

The C-Man, however, was not amused. "Okay, okay, knock it off right now. There's nothing funny about rape or murder—not the time or place for a bunch of juvenile jokes. This is serious, life and death stuff, and we've got to treat it that way."

Nick glanced around the newsroom. Clapper was right. All the investigators, including the journalists, were men. If women were working the case, it was not likely they'd be laughing. Okay, he could think of one woman—maybe two—who would toss out one-liners about the tiny penis tips. He punched Dave in the shoulder. "We've got a shitload of work to do. Let's find the killers and the rapists."

The two reporters started writing about what they'd witnessed. Tuesday's newspaper, they hoped, would include photos of the body parts, the box they'd come in, and the note. First edition press time was seven in the morning, and Clapper wanted to be ready for it.

Nick loved working all night on big stories, but Tanya not so much. He stepped away from the guys to call his new partner and give her an update. It was going to be another long night, and he wanted to brace her for it. Dave had to call no one. His girlfriend,

Natasha, was sleeping on the floor in Clapper's office under Dave's old army jacket.

The C-Man went to the office breakroom to make more coffee for those who would be coming in early. He also spent an hour dueling with the Bay City chief of police, who wanted the *Blade* editors to hold back some information from the newspaper report.

For example, the cops hoped they wouldn't mention that the two body parts in the box were penis tips. Such specific information would be known only by the killer. Same with describing the delivery package. Hold some detail back, they argued—which might help identify the killer.

Nick and Dave argued for full disclosure, and most of the *Blade* staff sided with the reporters. They did not think the newspaper should be playing footsie with the police. Report the news, they crowed. The *Blade* was now part of the story and all known details should be revealed. The newspaper's obligation, they said, was to its readers, not the police.

But the *Blade* management wanted to appear helpful, cooperative. They didn't want readers to think the paper was only interested in selling copies by printing salacious details instead of assisting in solving the crime.

A compromise was struck. The penis tips and package details were not mentioned in the *Blade* reporting for now, and authorities promised they would not disclose the information in press releases or interviews—the *Blade* would be the first news organization to reveal it.

What was clear to all parties was that the killers wanted the *Blade* involved.

"The assailants brought us into the story for a reason. This is our story. They want coverage, and I say let's give it to 'em," the C-Man told Nick. "Write everything we know and can verify. There are people out there in the community who know these killers. Let's try to get them to come forward. Push the story."

An extra copy editor, the photo chief, and a graphic designer were called in to develop a stellar package. Clapper also asked for more space to tell the story, ordering a four-page increase in the size of the paper.

Nick and Dave were impressed. The chief was fully engaged. Dave wondered aloud, "Do you think it's the caliber of the reporting? Or the fact that we finally got him to drink a beer in the newsroom?"

Chapter 6
Tuesday morning
Nick and Tanya's apartment

Nick's alarm, a bugler playing reveille, always got him moving regardless of how little sleep he'd had or how hung over he was. This morning it did the trick again. Tanya was already up and out of the shower when the horn blared. The newsman needed coffee, a shave, and a shower to get the day moving.

In a few hours he, Dave, and Anne would return to the Thumb. They wanted to talk to more families with missing persons, but also get updated information from authorities. Though they couldn't report it, the journalists were fascinated by the idea that they had been pulled into the story by the package with body parts and a note.

Tanya, who had been asleep when Nick got home at six in the morning, was eager to hear more about the delivery to the *Blade*. "Sounds like both tips were pretty small. Sure it wasn't toes or fingertips?" she asked.

"No, we're certain of what we saw. Even Quinn said something about them being little peckers. I think that, and Dave's comments, is what set the C-Man off. He ordered an end to what he called 'juvenile jokes,' which of course means we'll have to have Dave's jaw wired shut before this is over. Dave lives for this kind of stuff."

Tanya sided with the C-Man. "Clapper is right. You don't want to be seen as crude and insensitive when it comes to crimes like these. Not funny at all to victims or the families of victims."

Nick knew Tanya was—again—correct. Sensitivity was key for this reporting project. And with the possibility of a serial killer at work, the stakes in the story had risen.

Nick had called Booger right before eleven at night as the rural lawman drained his fifth beer of the evening. The deputy was shocked to learn of the package, but it convinced him that this case was getting bigger by the minute. And he'd had one request of Nick. "When CNN gets here, send Anderson Cooper directly to me. I got a couple of things I want to relate to Andy. Nobody else from CNN will do, it's got to be the big dog."

Tanya burst into the bathroom and gave Nick a kiss on the lips, saying she would catch up to him later. She was teaching third-graders at McKinley Elementary this semester and wanted to set up a special project before the youngsters showed up in her classroom.

"Will you be home for dinner?" she asked. "Should I take something out to toss in the oven, or are we going to wing it again?"

Nick could not give her an honest answer, but he didn't want to fly blind. That usually meant heating up cold pizza or leftovers from the weekend. "Don't know what the day will bring," he said, finishing his shave and wiping the edges of his lathered face. "I'll shoot you a note as soon as I get a sense of what we will be doing."

He hugged her tightly, then wiped shaving cream from her chin as she turned to leave for school. They were still honeymooning as far as he was concerned. It had been five months since they'd gotten married in Key West, and they were still enjoying each other—completely.

Mrs. Babcock, Nick's landlord and a retired real estate broker, had promised to help the couple buy a house after they saved up enough dough for a down payment. For now, Nick's tiny two-bedroom efficiency apartment was snug and comfy enough for the two of them. Most of Tanya's clothes and personal items were still at her mother's house.

Nick snagged an apple to go with the piece of toast slathered in peanut butter that Tanya had made for him. As he slid into the front seat of his vintage Pontiac Firebird, his cell phone pinged—a text message from Booger. "Medical examiner says two victims, white men in their thirties, checking to see if penis tips are a match, still sifting for teeth, not much more info. No clothing or personal effects found in field. Figures body tissue in field for several months, up to a year. May have found partial thumbprint but badly damaged. Heading for farm field and the shrine."

The deputy's text excited Nick—not a lot of new detail, but the possible thumbprint was fuel for the reporting engine that roared inside of Nick and kept him churning. He would press the ME for more details too. Even a crumb or two of additional information could end up being a new lead in this kind of story.

The reporter stopped at the *Blade* building to speak with Trudy in Classified, who was on duty when the penis package was dropped. She was in a group of *Blade* employees gathered around a coffee pot, whispering about the package and the articles that were being published by the rumbling presses in the basement as they spoke.

"Trudy, can I talk with you for a few minutes?" Nick asked. They had been coworkers for several years and knew each other well enough to say hello. "Need to pick your brain some more about the delivery guy."

"Sure thing. I already told the guard on duty and the police what I know," she said, walking toward Nick. "Young guy, Bay City Central hoodie, acne. Said to give the package to you and walked back out. That's it."

The reporter pressed ahead. "Have you seen him around downtown before? Has he made deliveries to the *Blade* or other nearby businesses?"

Trudy paused, and Nick could almost hear the wheels in her mind turning. After a few moments, she spat out, "A bike. He had a bike outside the front door. It had one of those hot/cold bags attached to a box on the back fender. I think it had the logo for a sandwich shop over on Third, near Washington. I forget the name, but they make those humongous subs."

Nick thanked Trudy for her great memory and scooted five blocks to the Savage Sub Shop, which was already baking bread for lunch deliveries. The baker said the young guy Nick described wouldn't be in until eleven. Hoodie Guy's name was Greg Szemanski, and right now he could probably be found in class over at Central High.

Nick was familiar with the home of the Wolves. Tanya's dad had been a teacher and administrator at the school for years before he died. A Central High counselor was one of Tanya's former classmates and still a good friend. She agreed to help Nick meet Greg off campus with his mother's permission.

Greg was a senior and due to graduate in May. The Savage Sub Shop was one of his two part-time jobs. The two met at Grandpa Tony's, a legendary Bay City restaurant just south of Central on Columbus Avenue. They split a pizza and pop. Greg was shy and worried he might be in trouble.

Nick assured him he'd done nothing wrong. Turned out that Trudy was right—the poor kid had a horrible case of acne, and Nick sympathized with him. He'd dealt with that too in his youth.

"Do you remember the package you dropped at the *Blade* late yesterday afternoon?" Nick asked. "I need to find out who asked you to make the delivery. It's very important."

Greg bit his lower lip. "Don't know his name, but I've seen him around town some."

"What did he say about the package he gave you?" Nick asked, leaning in toward the young man to emphasize that he hung on every word coming from Hoodie Guy. "Any special instructions?"

Greg shook his head. "Gave me a fifty-dollar bill and asked me to give the package to you at the *Blade*. Package had to go to you—said you're the hot-shit reporter and you must receive it. That's it. You weren't in your office, so I left it at the front desk."

Nick asked for a description. Greg said the guy was tall and rangy, probably six-three or more, dark hair with a scraggly beard. Wore a dark suit with no tie, Greg continued, and had a slight accent, Scottish or Irish.

A note had come with the package, Nick said. "Did you write the note or did the guy who gave you the package write it?"

The Central senior hesitated, then said, "Your name was already on the package. When I found out you weren't around, I wrote, 'Give to Nick Steele' on a piece of paper. The clerk at the desk taped the note to the package, and I left."

Nick pulled his card out of his sports jacket pocket, scribbled on the back, and gave it to Greg. "Call me if you think of anything else," he said. "And on the back, you'll see the name of a good friend of mine. Doc Servino. He's the best dermatologist in town. Go see him, tell him I sent you."

Greg shook his head and stared at the floor. "Thanks, but I'm saving every penny for college, and my mom's health insurance probably won't cover it. If he's good, I'll bet he's expensive and we simply can't pay for it."

"Doc owes me a favor or two. I'll make sure your visits are covered. Go see him. He's good and a nice guy."

The two men shook hands. Greg went to his second job, and Nick headed for the Thumb.

Chapter 7
Tuesday, noon
Bay City, East Side

Natalie O'Brien folded the newspaper on her kitchen table and called her sister.

Kate recognized the incoming call and picked up on the third ring, not bothering with a greeting. "Did you see the *Blade* yesterday and this morning? They found some surprises," Kate said, chuckling and a bit breathless. She chose her words carefully. "We've got nothing to worry about. They can't trace it back to us."

"It's causing quite a stir, and I'm glad." Natalie lit a cigarette and blew a plume of smoke toward an open window. "We're sending a message. I want it to be loud and clear. Soon as I hang up, I'm going to check the news to see if they've got any new—ah, tips."

Kate laughed out loud. "Good one," she said. "Now they know we're not dicking around."

Natalie and Kate were three years apart, in their mid-thirties, with kids of their own. Their brother, Larry, was the oldest and now in his early forties, six years Kate's senior. The O'Briens wore their Irish heritage on their sleeves and loved living in a city that treated St. Patrick's Day like it was the biggest holiday of the year.

The O'Briens were tight except when it came to religion. As kids, they'd attended catechism classes and daily Mass together. Now Natalie's faith in the Church was still alive, but Kate's was on life support. She'd gone through an angry divorce with a cheating husband. It was so ugly that Kate Martin had changed her name back to O'Brien after the marriage disintegrated. She didn't trust men, including those who wore the white collar. Larry had been suspicious of Catholic clergy since childhood and viewed the Church's rituals as mumbo-jumbo. Larry became legendary among his teen peers when he knocked the hell out of a priest who touched his thigh after Mass one day. The beating was never reported to authorities, and Larry's dad was so pleased with his son that he bought him a new bike for his *Bay City Blade* paper route.

Natalie, on the other hand, had stuck with the Church—even through the clergy sexual abuse and cover-up scandals. She needed it. The Church had been her rock when her husband was killed in a firefight in Afghanistan. The Church stood strong for her as she and her kids rebuilt their life and started in a new direction. Natalie had no doubt her siblings would not look kindly on the idea of her going to confession and spilling their sworn secret about the murders.

Before hanging up, Natalie reminded her older sister of their meeting later that day. More body parts needed to be spread, more messages sent, and other targets discussed with their leader, whom they only knew as Dr. Y. Kate and Natalie kidded each other that the single initial was short for "Yes," as in "Hell, yes, we're going to kill men who don't deserve to continue living."

Both women were committed to that—going after and taking down predators. Natalie wanted a better world for her daughters to grow up in, and she vowed she would do what it took to accomplish it. She checked her watch. Her daughters—aged eight and eleven—would be getting out of school in a couple of hours.

Natalie flicked on the radio in time for the WSGW broadcast. The host's voice sounded hurried and a tad higher when he launched his news report:

"Bay City Police are investigating an anonymous package containing two body parts and a note that were dropped off at the *Bay City Blade* sometime Monday afternoon. The package and note arrived after body tissue, chopped up into small chunks, was discovered in a Thumb farm field early Monday. Police fear the murder, or murders, may be the work of a serial killer. More after this word from our sponsors."

The report brought a smile to Natalie's lips. She released another cloud of smoke and jabbed her Virginia Slim in the air to emphasize her point. "Come on, man, tell 'em what kind of body parts were in the package and what the note said."

When more detail was not forthcoming, disappointment grew until it gave her a headache. It had been Natalie's idea, after all, to secure the penis tips after the executions and preserve them. They had sat frozen stiff in her kitchen freezer for more than a year. Her plan was to use the tips to send a graphic message if authorities discovered remains from any of their killings. "Stop the rapes" was their goal. Kate and Larry had gone along with Natalie, though reluctantly—they feared it was too dramatic and might end up leading to their capture. Still, Natalie persuaded them this could draw high-profile attention to the growing number of violent assaults on women. She hoped that bringing the *Blade* into the story in such a dramatic and horrific way would spark a public outcry so resounding that new laws and additional resources would be committed to ending the violence.

Finally Natalie switched off the radio and focused on collating the reports piled on her coffee table: a dozen fat files chock full of details about unsolved rapes in Bay City, Saginaw, Flint, and Midland. More importantly, the files contained the names and profiles of twelve rapists, Natalie's Dirty Dozen.

Two of the men would become their next targets. Kate, Larry, and Dr. Y would decide tonight which two would be killed and when the executions would take place. They would also decide when and where to distribute the body parts that were already chilling in a garage refrigerator in the Thumb.

Thank the Lord for Larry's friends, the guys he had met when working on farms during summers as a teen. They had taught Larry everything they knew, from tilling the fields to harvesting and slaughtering deer. Their lessons, experience, and knowledge about the most remote parts of the Thumb had become invaluable to a man bent on getting revenge and justice for his sister.

Natalie stacked the reports in a box and locked them in a hallway closet. She certainly did not want her girls, or the prying eyes of snoopy neighbors, to see them.

The twelve reports were spread out on Natalie's kitchen table when Kate rang the front doorbell. It was just after nine in the evening, and Natalie's daughters were finishing their homework in the bedroom the girls shared. House rule: lights out by ten on school nights.

Before Natalie could answer the door, Kate burst through, followed by their brother, Larry. Each carried a bottle of wine, lubricant that would get them through the process of selecting their targets—which they considered their most important and fulfilling task.

Natalie poured three glasses of wine as Kate and Larry settled in with the reports. They were already familiar with the cases and the rapists. Tonight they'd discuss their top four, then narrow the finalists down to two. Dr. Y would call about eleven, and the siblings would hand over their deliberations.

To be sure, the trio had no shortage of candidates. Each year, more than five thousand women in Michigan report rape to authorities. Roughly a third of those cases remain unsolved. And the experts who track sexual assault say a third of all rapes are never even reported. Natalie had not reported her assault, but her family considered the case solved when the remains of her assailants were spread in the Thumb farm field.

Kate started. She gave a quick summary of each of the four

nominated for final elimination. She singled out the Beyer assault three years earlier in Midland, the Dahlstrom assault in Flint two years earlier, the Tomlinson assault in Bay City that year, and the Orginsky assault in Saginaw the year before.

Natalie was the lead investigator on the Beyer assault. She summarized: Susan Beyer had been working late on a cool October evening in 2011. As she fumbled with her keys in the parking lot, she was attacked by Randy Cobb, who had stalked her for weeks. Cobb held her captive for days, assaulting her repeatedly. She escaped when her assailant passed out from drinking. Devastated, Beyer had not reported the assault for a week. Meanwhile, Cobb disappeared. The motel had accepted cash for the room, which had been cleaned twice and rented by the time the cops arrived to look for evidence of a crime.

Larry shuddered as he reread the file. Susan Beyer had suffered multiple injuries during the assault, and it had turned her life upside down. She'd lost her job because depression made it too hard for her to leave home.

Kate agreed with Natalie and Larry. The Beyer assault was horrible, and Randy Cobb should forfeit his life for it. During their investigation of Cobb, they'd discovered that he and his crew were prime suspects in a series of Midland rapes. Police, however, feared they did not have enough evidence to convict, and charges were never filed.

When Larry found Cobb, he was stalking another Midland woman in the same parking lot where he had laid out Susan Beyer with a brick. Larry photographed Cobb. When shown the photo, Susan Beyer had no problem identifying him as the man who had kidnapped and tortured her.

"Any doubts about Randy Cobb?" Natalie asked, studying her siblings' faces. She asked for a Roman Senate signal on the verdict.

"Thumbs up, he survives another round, down, and we take him out."

Three thumbs at the kitchen table were thrust into the air and then turned downward. Randy Cobb's report went to the kill pile.

The trio reviewed three more reports. By a quarter to eleven, Sean Davis of Flint had joined Cobb in the pile of the doomed. The threesome agreed that his assault on Lisa Dahlstrom, a freshman at Flint Southwestern Academy, qualified him for elimination.

Davis had pulled Lisa into his van as she walked home from school. Later he dumped her—barely breathing—behind the skeletal remains of Buick City in Flint's north end. The police could not locate Davis and his van, but Larry had little difficulty finding both. Lisa said the red van had a picture of a giant wrench with the slogan "No job too small" and a phone number. It also had a General Motors parking lot sticker on the windshield, allowing Davis to park at the Chevy truck plant. Larry put a GPS tracker on the gas tank of the van as it sat in the parking lot. After work, Davis led Larry to his home, which had an active landline with the phone number on the van.

Lisa, distraught from the attack and shunned at school, had spiraled downward. Her parents did their best to help her, but she finally dropped out and then overdosed on her mom's pain meds.

When Natalie saw all three thumbs in the air pointing down, Sean Davis hit the kill pile.

The siblings had one last item of business. They needed to decide where and when to dump the body they had cooling in a garage refrigerator in the Thumb. The body had belonged to Ted Ferrier, a nomad who roamed the country picking up jobs for cash where he could. He'd also left a trail of rapes in his path.

"I've got a good location for a dump," Larry said. "It's a hundred-year-old stone quarry less than forty miles from here. It's a limestone strip mine, but one section has a nice pit. They won't be mining again for another month, so the body tissue won't be discovered for a while."

Natalie and Kate trusted their big brother. They nodded in agreement.

"Don't forget to save Ted's tip," Kate said, pushing her hand in the air with two fingers two inches apart. "Dump him when you think it's safe, then we'll send out a message after he's discovered." She drained her glass and stood at the table. "It's almost eleven. Ready to send the signal?"

Natalie opened her laptop and sent out an encrypted email, which signaled Dr. Y to call Kate on her fifty-seven-dollar Nokia burner cell phone. The call lasted five minutes. Davis and Cobb were scheduled for execution—time, date, and place the choice of Dr. Y. Larry would receive a text message on his Samsung burner to pick up the bodies for disposal.

Natalie checked on her daughters as Kate boxed up the rape reports. Larry rinsed the wine glasses. As the siblings hugged before parting ways, Natalie wished Kate and Larry good fortune by whispering in their ears, "Happy killing!"

The trio high-fived.

Chapter 8
Wednesday morning
Bay City Blade newsroom

Nick worked feverishly to finish his story for that day's midmorning edition. His article focused on how the two victims whose remains were found in the farm field had died. He skimmed his notes and recalled the interviews he'd conducted Tuesday afternoon and evening.

Albert DeRossier, an MD who also served as medical examiner for Huron, Tuscola, and Sanilac Counties, had spoken with Nick at great length in his office in Bad Axe. He believed the victims were killed in another location, frozen for an undetermined length of time, and then dumped in the field with natural fertilizer several months back. When the owner of the farm field decided to have it tilled, the body tissue had popped out of the ground and become snacks for the gulls.

"I think the body tissue was mixed and buried with manure to speed decomposition," DeRossier said, flipping through the pages of his initial report. The doc wore a white lab coat and was as thin as an exclamation point. His gray hair was bushy with a fresh-fried look, like he'd stuck a screwdriver into an electrical outlet. "The bones show they were sawed to pieces—like the bodies were repeatedly pushed through a commercial saw. No doubt about it, the kill site would be messy, with a wide spray pattern. Bone fragments and tissue flying everywhere."

Nick asked about teeth. Why hadn't the officers sifting the field found any teeth among the remains? Doc indicated the teeth were either pulled or knocked out of the upper and lower jawbones, an effort to conceal their identities, he believed. Nick grimaced at the

41

thought as he jotted notes.

What about a toxicology report? Nick wondered if any drugs were detected.

"Initial findings didn't show evidence of alcohol, but we did see trace elements of cocaine," he told Nick. "But we're going deeper, though it may not mean much."

"What about the partial thumb that was found—enough for a print? Any luck?" Nick asked.

The ME shook his head no, his gray frizz shimmying side to side. "Sent to the FBI—got my fingers crossed. If this guy was fingerprinted at some point, that'd be a big break for us."

The reporter had also talked with a neighboring farmer who claimed to have witnessed unusual activity in the farm field during the last year. Nick found the farmer tending hogs in a small barn and adjoining fenced yard behind his two-story home.

Aaron Schmidt, who lived a half mile from where the body tissue was discovered, put his slop bucket down and wiped his hands on his faded jeans. He was as big as a plow horse, with thick, hairy hands. A healthy crop of chest hair sprouted through his open collar and made his neck look like he was wearing a hair scarf. A green-and-yellow John Deere ballcap was balanced atop his black crew cut.

Nick shook his calloused paw and knew immediately that Aaron was a man who worked with his hands all day.

"This is the result of some damn kids courting the devil," said the farmer, who rented out much of his land to dairy farmers. "We see bonfires out here at all hours of the night. They play loud music, they get drunk, they chant, they couple—and who knows what else goes on out there? You start looking into those kids, and you'll find your killers."

When the reporter asked for evidence that kids might be involved in the deaths, Hairy Hands grunted and waved him off.

Nick said he would look into the farmer's theories and asked if he had anything else to add for the interview.

"If it ain't the kids, then it's got to be the aliens," Schmidt said, returning to the slop bucket. That caught Nick's attention because of the articles he'd written on folks commonly referred to as illegal aliens, or undocumented workers from Mexico.

"Are you saying illegal aliens working the dairy farms had a hand in this?" Nick asked, moving closer to Hairy Hands to make sure he understood.

"Ah, no. Not illegal aliens." Schmidt dumped a lumpy gruel into the hog feeder. A glob bounced out of the feeder and covered his right boot. He continued unfazed while a hungry hog shined his boot with its tongue. "I'm talking the kind from above. From space machines. We got a guy lives down the road who claims he was abducted and flown away for questioning in one of their ships. Torture, sexual abuse, brainwashing. You name it, they did it to him. Want his phone number? The wife's got it just inside the house."

Nick didn't.

Everyone, it seemed, had theories about the body tissue found in the field, but real evidence in the case was hard to come by. The tip lines still buzzed with activity. Four different men in Huron County were flagged by their ex-wives as monsters capable of the killings and other hideous crimes. Deputies checked each one out with no luck and concluded the ex-husbands were despicable and lowdown dirty dogs but not murderers.

Dave had chased down leads from the *Blade*'s tip line: possible suspects with suspicious pasts, noisy neighbors who came and went at all hours of the night, and a group of teens from Garber High School who were accused of practicing witchcraft. One Bay City woman even claimed she'd overheard a Catholic confession in which someone acknowledged killing two people. Dave had been unable to reach her. So far, he had come up with nothing.

Meanwhile, Sheriff Donaldson clung to his theories of a mob or gangland hit. "I think some kids who picked up on the original story decided to have fun with the newspaper," he said, laughing off the fact that the county medical examiner had already confirmed the penis tips matched the tissue in the field. "Not a serial killer, just a plain, old-fashioned rubout."

The sheriff was much more concerned with the shrine next to the site where the tissue was discovered. Crowds were showing up to pray, sing hymns, light candles, and leave messages with flowers and balloons. Folks were rolling in from all over Michigan and beyond, many of them purely gawkers.

To commemorate the event, a bar in nearby downtown Caseville was offering a drink and food special: the Corpse Reviver on ice and a hot Body Bag sandwich, $9.95. Though callous and crude, the combo was a big hit among locals and visitors to the area.

Tensions at the shrine had escalated. At one point, a fight had broken out between a local group of mourners and a van full of folks who had traveled from Toronto when the story broke. The Canadians started planting national flags at the shrine. Thumb residents took exception to it and burned the flags. National anthems blared amid pushing and shoving and name-calling. The whole incident lasted less than an hour, but it gave locals and foreigners something to yack about for days.

Deputy Ratchett had separated the groups before handguns were drawn. No need to see more bodies stack up.

Besides, Booger had his hands full with the national media flocking to the region. He'd told Nick he was crushed to learn that CNN had sent a flunky into Michigan farm country to cover the story. "Can you believe it? Just when we get a blockbuster story going, they send the B team. And they are rude and pushy. Wish

Andy was here."

Nick had tried to explain the practicality of news coverage. He was surprised CNN had sent anybody. Most of the time, the big news outlets simply picked up a newsfeed from one of the local TV stations. "They don't send the high-priced talent until it's a worthy story. But the cable executives must already think this could be substantial."

As Nick was finishing his interviews Tuesday, a wildly colored tie-dyed van had inched up close to the shrine. Lettering on the side spelled out "Madame Charmane, Psychic Medium, Port Austin." When the vehicle stopped, a small crowd gathered near the side door, and out stepped a woman who Nick guessed was pushing seventy-five. She was dressed in long, flowing purple and yellow linens, and a red scarf held back a mop of coarse, untamed white hair. If she'd been younger, she would have looked like a Minnesota Vikings cheerleader.

Booger let out a moan. "Oh no, not Crazy Charmane. Sit back and relax, Nick, this should be good!"

Madame Charmane dropped to her knees in the mud and clutched her head with both hands. She chanted in a low voice, the volume increasing with each repetition. Nick struggled to make out the words. At one point, he thought she was chanting in Latin. Booger said it was gibberish.

The crowd formed a circle around her and joined her incantations, hoping for a connection to spirits on the other side. The driver of her van moved among them, handing out cards that advertised her psychic readings—twenty-five dollars each—on Saturday mornings during the Port Austin Farmer's Market. The back of her card declared she was also an artist who made jewelry and sold it through the Cove, a retail outlet in Port Austin that featured one-of-a-kind handcrafted works created by local artists.

Suddenly Madame Charmane rose to her feet, raised her hands in the air, and declared that she had made a connection with the spirits of the deceased in the adjoining field. "The spirits are speaking. They wish to be heard. They want justice. They want vengeance."

And with that, she collapsed on the ground, her body falling limply into the mud. The crowd gasped as one. Charmane's driver held her head up from the gooey slop. Her lips were moving, but her voice barely whispered. The driver lowered his head to hear. "She's okay but exhausted by her journey into the beyond. Madame Charmane will conduct a séance tonight in the meeting room at the Cove. Only those with clean minds and souls may attend. Fifty dollars each at the door. Seven o'clock."

Booger turned to Nick and deadpanned, "You goin' to the séance?"

"Don't think I qualify for admittance to the show."

"Ha," Boog hooted. "That's what this is becoming. A show."

Chapter 9
Wednesday afternoon
Kilmanagh

As Michigan ghost towns went, the hamlet of Kilmanagh was typical. It rested wearily between the villages of Sebewaing and Bay Port, a few miles from Saginaw Bay and Lake Huron. A handful of aging buildings still struggled to remain erect, but the town was nowhere close to the bustling hub it had been a century ago.

Only a handful of residents now called Kilmanagh home. These days the town was a destination for photographers to capture images of forlorn buildings decaying from time and the elements.

Larry O'Brien kept a close eye on the rearview mirror as he steered his van through what was once a vibrant downtown. No sign of cops—county or state—running a speed trap. A youngster on a bike with training wheels stopped in front of the old general store and watched Larry's vehicle crawl through town. Otherwise, Kilmanagh seemed deserted. The only things missing, he thought, were rolling tumbleweed and the sound of a baying coyote.

It was just as he remembered it from high school, when he worked on farms surrounding the tiny village. He thought about those days while inching down Bay Port Road. When he passed the hollow remnants of Kelly's Bar, he tipped his cap to his old man.

Larry's dad, Kevin, was an Irish immigrant and had approved of his son working in Kilmanagh. Kevin had told Larry that farm work would make him tough and hard, the kind of young man who'd look out for his younger sisters, Natalie and Kate. Kevin's rule number one: Never allow your sisters to be trifled with. They were not to be bullied, taunted, or dishonored in any way.

That rule was reinforced when necessary with Kevin's belt

across Larry's backside. This did make the younger O'Brien tough and hard but also gave him a vicious mean streak. One day, when a sixth-grader made the mistake of snapping Natalie's bra strap in study hall, Larry beat the kid with his fists so badly, the kid ended up with an ambulance trip to the hospital. The message was clear. Don't mess with the O'Brien girls, or Larry would literally knock the, ah, urine, out of you.

Soon the intersection with Shebeon Road came into view. Larry headed south on the dusty gravel road, keeping one eye on the rearview mirror and the other on the lookout for his landmark. A large oak tree, split down the middle by a lightning strike, marked the entrance to an abandoned homestead set a half mile off the road.

At the end of the drive, a two-story house with broken windows and rotting gray clapboard leaned away from prevailing winds. The house, now home to marauding racoons, had not been lived in by humans for decades. A dozen years earlier, the barn had been reclaimed by Amish carpenters and was now decorative trim in trendy townhouses in the city.

Two other outbuildings located behind the house had so far escaped the fate of the barn. Weathered dark gray, the ancient granary and storage shed flanked an old-fashioned windmill with its wheel and paddles still spinning in the northerly wind.

Larry parked the van behind the granary in chest-high weeds. Inside, he stopped to listen for critters nesting in, or under, the old building. His flashlight beam swept across the open space until it landed on a cabinet freezer, which hummed from a stack of batteries hooked up to the windmill.

The place looked untouched since he'd stuffed Ted in the freezer more than a month before. Larry breathed heavily. He hung the flashlight from a nail above the freezer and opened the lid.

While alive, Ted had been a big man. Now he was reduced to

four plastic bags, each weighing roughly fifty pounds. To anyone else, the contents of the clear plastic bags looked like they could have been hamburger or processed deer meat.

Larry smiled—this dirtbag would never harm a woman again.

With some grunting and groaning, he moved the bags from the freezer to his van. The last task was plucking the small cardboard box from a tray inside the freezer. It contained Ted's weapon of choice in his war on women. Like the last box, it would be sent to the hotshot reporter—Nick Steele—with a message after Ted's remains were discovered.

Larry waited for daylight to fade, then headed north toward the dump site. Easy does it, he told himself, plenty of time to finish the day's business. No reason to speed or draw attention to the van.

Within ten minutes of turning back onto Bay Port Road, Larry noticed a sedan some distance behind him, becoming larger by the second. Larry thought it was a Chevy but couldn't quite tell. He did his best not to wobble on the road, steering straight and true. Then a light bar on its roof and the searchlight on the driver's side door became clear. It was unmistakable. Cop car.

Larry's stomach rolled. He told himself to remain calm and in control. Cops patrolled these country roads all the time, looking for speeders and teens out splitting a six-pack. No big deal. He wasn't driving too fast or drinking. Breathe deep and exhale.

The Huron County Sheriff's Deputy cruiser slowed as it approached. Larry gripped the steering wheel so tightly, he thought his knuckles might pop through his skin. His mind raced. Were his plate tags expired? Did he have a broken taillight? Was he driving too slowly? Was he suspicious?

The cruiser clung to the van like a stripper hanging onto a pole. Larry used a forefinger to brush light beads of sweat from his forehead. Now what? Should he slow down more or speed up?

Look for a place to turn off the road?

Flashing lights almost made Larry's heart stop. He put his turn signal on and pulled over. As he reached for his registration and license in the glove box, he glanced into the back of the van, glad he'd covered the plastic bags and small box with a blanket. For a second he toyed with the idea of adjusting the blanket, but he resisted the impulse. He did not want to draw attention to it or what it covered.

The deputy took what seemed like forever to reach the side window, which Larry had already rolled down.

"Is there a problem, officer?"

"Well, howdy there. How you doin' today?" the deputy said, leaning down and scanning the inside of the van. Larry checked the cop's name tag: "J.R. Ratchett."

"Doing pretty darned good," Larry said, smiling, acting as happy-go-lucky as he could. "Did I do something wrong?"

"Now, I ain't goin' to write you up for this, but your brake lights are out." The cop glanced toward the rear of the van. "Thought you should know. The next officer might not be so forgiving."

Larry's shoulders went limp with relief. "Oh, wow. Didn't realize I had a light out. I'll get it fixed right away. Thanks, Deputy Ratchett!"

"Just call me Booger. Everybody does. You from around here?"

"Bay City. Thought I'd check the fishing at Mud Creek—it's my favorite spot. Fished it since I was a kid. What do you hear, Booger? Are the perch biting? How about walleye?"

J.R. put his hands on his hips and looked north toward the bay. "Always good in the spring when the ice comes off. You can't go wrong at Mud Creek."

Larry said he hoped to get there before dark, hinting for the deputy to let him be on his way. It worked.

"Well, I won't hold you up. Drive safe. Catch you later."

Larry grunted a laugh. "Hope not."

The two parted ways, with J.R. speeding ahead of the van. Larry was so delighted with his good luck that he almost cried out. But he knew he had to do two things immediately: get rid of the body parts in the back and find a new place to dump them.

After encountering the deputy, Larry believed it was risky to dump Ted's remains at a site on the same road where he'd been stopped. He drove by the quarry entrance on Bay Port Road, slowing to think about his next move. Kate was their ringleader, he reasoned—she would know.

But Kate, in fact, did not know what to do next. "This part is your job. Don't you have a backup plan?"

That ticked Larry off. True, he was the older brother and had agreed to handle the dirty work for his sisters. He would do anything for them. But now he'd stumbled and he needed assistance. While trying not to say too much on the phone about his predicament, he pleaded for ideas—something, anything to get out of this tough spot.

Kate said she needed to clear her head and think. She urged him to get off the road until they had figured it out. Larry turned the van west onto M-25, and within minutes he'd parked his van in a lonely spot near the Bay Port Inn, a local watering hole.

Inside, he ordered a black coffee, which was met with a quizzical look from the waitress.

"We don't get too many orders for coffee this time of day," she said with a smile. "Do you want me to spice it up a bit, maybe an Irish coffee?"

Larry scanned the bar. Two other patrons, both pounding down draft beers. "I'll take what they're drinking, and how about a menu?"

White foam from the golden lager oozed over the lip of the mug. Larry, who had never been much of a drinker thanks to the excesses of his old man, spun the beer with his fingers. The frosty mug was slowly warming.

Suddenly it occurred to him to check on the van.

"Oh shit, shit," he shrieked. Nine stray dogs—every loose mutt in Bay Port—were circling the van. A trickle of light-pink liquid dripped from the rear door. Ted was thawing.

Larry tossed a ten-spot on the table and slipped out of the bar, hoping not to draw any more attention to himself.

As he pulled away from the Bay Port Inn, the mutts followed, yipping as they pranced alongside the vehicle. The canines acted like they were chasing a meat wagon, which in reality it was. Larry could not speed on a residential street. As he passed the town's post office and bank, an older lady with a cane dropped her mail at the sight of the dogs, their number now increased to thirteen. Larry turned left on M-25 and drove toward Caseville, still not sure what he would do with Ted.

What now? His mind spun wildly. He passed the old Bay Port Cemetery and briefly toyed with the idea of burying Ted in the sandy soil, but the only tool he had with him was a jack handle. And he was all but certain someone passing by would spot him digging. Not a good look, especially as dusk turned to the blackness of a moonless night.

His cell buzzed. It was Kate. "I've got the perfect spot," she said, sounding as excited as if she'd hit the lottery. "If you're heading toward Caseville, keep going."

Larry clicked off his phone and checked his mirrors again. No sign of yapping dogs on his trail and no sign of cops. He waited for Kate to send him the location for a dump site. Driving around with a body in the back was becoming stressful. If he and his sisters were to continue with the Vigilant Vigilantes, he would have to come up with a better method of disposal.

Chapter 10
Wednesday afternoon
Bay City, South End

Dave Balz maneuvered his green '95 Chevy pickup down Lincoln Street. As he neared the intersection with Cass Avenue, he spotted the home of Andrea Pilinski. She sat on a porch swing in the April sunshine, bundled up in a gold down-filled coat and a red knit hat with matching mittens. She smiled and waved as Dave's jalopy slowed to a sputtering stop next to her driveway.

The reporter introduced himself and thanked her for meeting him. She invited him inside for coffee next to the fireplace.

"I love sitting in the spring sunshine, but you've got to be prepared for it," she said, noting Dave's ratty-looking red-and-brown-checked sports jacket, black jeans, and multicolored necktie complete with fading chili dog and mustard stains. If she hadn't expected him, she might have mistaken Dave for a homeless man driving a junk truck.

Dave had already shoved his hands in his pockets for warmth. He eagerly thanked her for the invitation and nodded toward his pickup. "Mrs. Pilinski, a friend came with me today. Would you mind if she joined us during the interview?"

The woman looked back at Dave's truck and smiled. "Why, no, not at all. Please introduce me to your friend."

Dave put two fingers to his lips and whistled, two short bursts. The truck door opened and out popped Natasha, her smile as bright as the spring sunshine. A blue knit hat with a fuzzy tassel bobbed on her head, covering light-brown hair just starting to gray. She wore a blue jean jacket and tan corduroy pants. Pointed cowboy boots completed the look.

"Hi, Mrs. Pilinski, I've heard so much about you. I'm glad to meet you," the younger woman said, sticking out her tiny mitt. "Please call me Tasha, my friends do."

The grandmother grabbed her hand with both of hers and led her ahead of Dave into her tidy two-story bungalow. "Your hands are cold, my dear. We've got to get you warmed up."

The older woman seated them next to the fireplace, which crackled with split dry pine. Family photos adorned the walls. A billowy flower-covered couch sat squarely in front of a television perched in the center of a wooden entertainment center.

Andrea retreated to the kitchen to bring out a tray of coffee and cookies.

The moment she disappeared, Tasha leaned into Dave's ear. "Next time you whistle for me, I'm going to clock you a good one. I'm not a collie. Don't do it again."

Dave started to protest but realized it was futile. Instead he whispered, "I'm sorry. That was awful. I'm such a clod."

She winked. "But you're a cute clod," she said, rising to help Mrs. Pilinski with the tray. The reporter's eyes lit up at the sight of the cookies, which he considered one of the major food groups. One of his favorite sayings was "Man may not be able to live on cookies alone, but it would be a helluva lot of fun trying."

"I love oatmeal and raisin!" Dave pushed back his bushy brown hair with both hands before digging into the treats. The coffee, an aromatic French roast, filled the room, giving it a homey, comfortable feel.

Dave addressed her as Mrs. Pilinski, respectful of her age. He guessed she was nearly thirty years his senior.

"Please call me Andrea," their host said. Her weather gear now removed, she displayed silver-blond curls, rosy cheeks, and full lips that did not require painting. She plopped her short, stocky frame squarely in a rocker across from Dave, her buckskin moccasins barely touching the floor. "How can I help you?"

The reporter pulled out his notebook and pen. "As I mentioned on the phone, I'm following up on your call to the tip line we set up for leads on the bodies discovered out in the Thumb. You indicated you heard something in church."

"To be honest, I'm not totally sure what I heard, but what I thought I picked up was so jarring, I decided I should report it." She blew on her coffee and took three quick sips. "I hope you don't think I'm crazy or some kind of nut job."

Dave thought she seemed nervous, not unusual for someone who rarely gave interviews or spoke with reporters. He tried to put her at ease. "No, not at all," Dave said, balancing his notebook on his thigh as he scribbled. "We're trying to check out all the tips that come into the office, and yours sounded interesting. Yours sounded sane."

The reporter double-checked the spelling of her name and asked Andrea for some basic information. She obliged, saying she was a retired nurse from Bay Medical Center. She and her late husband, Ralph, had reared three beautiful children in the home on Lincoln, and now she was blessed with seven grandchildren. Andrea pointed out their photos on the walls, offering a quick narrative of their successes and exploits.

Tasha nodded approvingly and told Andrea her mom had been a nurse, twenty-five years in the emergency room.

Dave took it all in, not wanting to rush Andrea. She seemed talkative and bright—he didn't sense that she was losing her marbles. He hoped this level of enthusiasm would carry over into their interview.

It did.

"What exactly did you hear in church?" he asked when the

conversation between the women slowed.

Andrea put her cup down and coughed lightly into her hand. She explained how Father Bob and St. Clementine's offered confessions on Mondays, Wednesdays, and Fridays, and that she went every Monday night to light a candle for Ralph and take advantage of the confessional.

Last Monday, she continued, had started out the same as always—a half hour by herself in prayer and reflection. She'd prayed for Ralph, she said, reciting in low tones the nicest things she could remember about him.

"When I turned around, I saw a woman I didn't recognize, and I know almost everyone in our parish, don't you know," she said, her head swiveling between Dave and Tasha. "Well, I couldn't place her, but that's okay—we're open to all who want to celebrate the sacraments, don't you know."

Dave nodded and asked her to continue. "What happened next?"

"I saw her go into the confessional. I stopped to say hello to the Andersons, then I went into the open booth. That's when you gather your final thoughts before confessing, don't you know."

"No, I don't," Dave said, still jotting notes. "I'm not Catholic, but I'm fascinated by the process. I've gotta ask. In those quiet moments of reflection, can you hear what the priest is saying to the other person confessing?"

"Usually just faint whispers. But Monday night was different, because the woman raised her voice. She said she wasn't remorseful and she cursed, and that's not something you hear in the confessional." Andrea had inched forward in her rocker, her toes almost touching the floor, and her voice gained urgency.

"Cursed? Can you give me a clue?" Dave asked.

"Oh, I couldn't repeat the word. It hurts me to think of it. But

I'll give you a hint: the first letter of the word is *H* and it ends in double hockey sticks." Andrea smiled, quite pleased with her communication of the bad word. Dave chuckled loudly, and Andrea put down her coffee. "Well, what she said next—I remember it like she said it five minutes ago. She told Father Bob she was sorry about lying, card cheating, and cursing—but the killing of walking, talking vermin, she said no and used the double-hockey-sticks word again, don't you know." Andrea used her elbows on the arms of the chair to lift herself back into her seat as though she had just concluded a closing argument.

Dave thought she was either very credible or a fantastic liar. Could what she was saying be true? He had the sense that she was right on the money, but he needed to push.

Before he could ask his next question, Tasha leaned forward and clasped Andrea's hands, saying that what she heard must have been traumatic. Andrea closed her eyes and prayed quietly, leaning toward Tasha. Dave half expected her to tumble off the rocker onto her knees, but the woman held firm at the edge of the chair. The reporter gave her a few moments and collected his thoughts.

When she relaxed and looked up, he restarted the interview. "I'm surprised you were able to continue after hearing those horrible words. How did you go on with your own confession?"

"It wasn't easy, but I stayed focused," she said, picking up her coffee cup and blowing over the black liquid. "Father Bob spoke like everything was normal. But I heard him tell her it would be a terrible burden to carry the sin with her, don't you know."

Again, Dave didn't, but he wanted her to keep going. He could tell Andrea was winding down even though she seemed relieved to tell her story, like it'd been weighing on her. Now she suddenly looked tired.

He nudged her along. "I'll bet it was quite distressing for you to hear that, to take it all in. I understand this has not been easy for you, and I appreciate your candor. I have one more question for you. Did you ask Father Bob about what you'd overheard?"

Andrea paused before responding in a low voice, like she was revealing a secret to a friend. "Yes, I did. After I finished my confession and Father Bob gave me absolution and penance, I asked if I could continue speaking with him in confidence. He said yes but told me the confessional was sacred and that anything someone might think they overheard was probably not accurate and should not be repeated. I said I understood."

Dave let that soak in for a moment. "Obviously he knows you overheard at least part of the confession. So, I'm curious. Why did you call us if he asked you not to repeat it?"

"I'm not a priest," she said, standing up as if to emphasize what was about to come. "Father Bob has his vows—he's not allowed to reveal what he hears in confession. I'm not bound by anything similar, and what I overheard was evil. No one has the right to be judge, jury, and executioner. That's the Lord's job. I felt I had an obligation—as a good person and a Christian—to speak up. I'm counting on you, Mr. Dave, to get this information in front of the right people. It would break my heart to think this woman might kill again. She was angry, not sorry in the least."

Dave told her he would do his best to spread the word—kind of like the gospels. She walked her guests to the door and thanked them for hearing her out.

As they left the home on Lincoln, Dave knew he had to fill in Nick and the C-Man, but he also understood they needed to find Father Bob for a chat. Perhaps the priest could help them without violating his vows. So far Andrea, the little old Polish woman, was the best lead they had.

Chapter 11
Late Wednesday afternoon
Bay City Blade newsroom

The features editor hovered over Nick's desk as the reporter wrapped up a telephone interview with the Huron County Medical Examiner. The doc still did not have a match on a print from the partial thumb discovered among the human remains, but expected a call from the lab at any time. Other than the possible print match, he had nothing new to share.

The features editor, an aging bleach blonde as thin as a knife's edge, stood directly across from Nick with her arms folded. The reporter could not tell if she was tapping her foot, but he guessed her toes slapped the carpet furiously on the other side of his desk.

She waited for him to complete his call, then launched into him. "Nick, you are way past deadline on your part of the Madonna story. It's scheduled to run Sunday. Where is your work?" She almost spat out the words. "The artwork is done, the page layout is roughed in, the other reporters have finished their parts of the story, and—once again—we're waiting on the hotshot reporter."

Nick didn't care for the jab. He was still waiting on a call from Madonna's publicist in New York City, and he had his hands full covering the murders in the Thumb. "It's coming, it's coming," he said, exasperated. Breaking, developing news always trumped timeless feature stories. Everybody knew that except her, he thought. "Besides, I'll bet the murder update story for Sunday blows Madonna off the front page for another week—at least."

"Perhaps, but Madonna is still on the weekend news budget for Sunday," she said, adjusting her glasses as though that would give her declaration more clout. "Final deadline is Friday at noon. If you don't make it, I'm afraid I'll have to take this up with the publisher."

She whirled away, arms still folded. The threat didn't bother Nick. He and the publisher were on solid ground, especially after she'd sexually harassed him before he and Tanya married. Nick had captured her indecent and unlawful advances on tape. She knew it and steered clear of him whenever she could.

Nick was about to check in with the C-Man, when his cell phone pinged with a text message: "Got a print match to a man with a Grand Blanc address. Flint area police alerted. Get details from Booger."

Nick learned from the deputy that the print matched a Guy Devereaux, who had lived in a Grand Blanc subdivision that bordered the cities of Flint and Burton. But that was more than a year earlier. No forwarding address.

Nick called the townhouse manager, who did not have much to share. "I already told the cops what I know. Devereaux was evicted for nonpayment. Sheriff's deputies put his shit on the curb. His sister picked up two boxes of personal items. End of story."

"Do you have a number for the sister?" Nick asked. "Does she live in the area?"

Nick heard a file cabinet slam shut and papers rattle in the background. "Well, this number is from a while ago, so I can't vouch for it. Her name is Sandy and I have no idea where she lives."

Nick jotted it down and thanked the manager. A reverse number search revealed that Sandy was Sandra Stevenson and she lived in Saginaw, just a hop, skip, and long pole vault from Bay City.

Nick tried her number. She answered on the fifth ring, but when Nick identified himself, she hung up. He tried a second time, with the same result.

The C-Man walked past Nick's desk.

"Hey, chief, we got a match on that thumbprint. It's a guy from the Flint area who was evicted from his place for nonpayment after he disappeared. Timing is perfect for our remains in the Thumb. His sister lives in Saginaw. She hung up on me twice, so I'm going to visit her."

Clapper nodded. "Go track her down, Nick. This might be the big break we need."

Sandy's address took Nick deep into Kochville Township, an upscale, predominately white neighborhood north of Saginaw. Brick ranch homes with landscaped yards and neat sidewalks wound off into the distance. The reporter steered his rumbling Firebird down the street, passing Sandy's driveway. No vehicles, drapes closed, house dark and quiet.

A woman pushed a stroller past him, her two toddlers, bundled and feverishly working pacifiers, soaking up warm sunshine on their pink faces.

Nick rolled down his window. "Hello, I'm trying to locate one of your neighbors," he said, smiling and hoping he didn't scare the woman, who looked to be in her mid-twenties. "Would you happen to know a Sandra Stevenson?"

She stopped and thought for a moment. "Who wants to know?"

"I've got some information about her brother, whom she hasn't seen in quite a while," he said, one arm hanging out of his window and one hand on the wheel. He did his best to sound casual. He did not want to alarm her. "Just trying to connect with her to let her know."

The woman inched the stroller closer. The pacified youngsters focused on the stranger in the gold car, their jaws still working. She pointed to the ranch Nick had passed on the street. "Sandy lives right there. She keeps to herself. Good neighbor, except too many visitors."

Nick pulled into Sandy's driveway as the woman with the toddlers gave him side-eye. He waited until she had moved down the street, then approached the house.

The doorbell issued an ancient chime: *ding-dong!* Nick listened for activity from inside the house. Nothing. *Ding-dong!* This time, one of the drawn curtains shook and an eyeball peered through an opening between the blinds. Nick rang again.

"What do you want? I'm not buying anything. Go away," she commanded through the front door, which remained closed.

Nick raised his voice. "I've got some information about your brother. Thought you might want to know what happened to him."

Silence, then more rustling of the curtains. "Cops already told me he's dead. Go away."

"Don't you want to know how he died? Don't you want to find out why?"

"Don't care. Haven't seen him or his dickhead friend in years," Sandy said, her voice trailing off before she issued another command. "Please go away, and don't come back."

"I'm not going away until we have a chat. I will tell you everything I know, and you tell me what you know. It won't take more than five or six minutes, tops."

More silence. Nick was about to poke the doorbell again, when he heard the automatic garage door open. He walked toward it, half expecting a car to roll out. But there was no car in the garage. Taped boxes lined one wall. A bin overflowing with empty beer bottles and pop cans occupied a corner; filled trash bags, some spilling their contents, were piled to the ceiling in the other.

After a moment, the garage door to the house creaked open and a short, stocky woman stepped out. She wore a blue terrycloth bathrobe and old-school black tennis shoes. Curlers the size of orange juice cans bounced atop her head as she closed the door behind her with one hand and clutched the front of her robe with the other.

Nick identified himself and said he was looking into the death of her brother.

The woman shrugged. "I don't give a shit," she said, spit flying from her lips as she spoke. She had dark circles under her eyes, and her skin was ashen. "I told the cops when they called that I don't know anything about him and haven't for years. Now, leave me alone—P-L-E-A-S-E!"

"Did they tell you he was chopped up into bits, mixed with cow shit, and buried in a farm field? Did they tell you his penis was clipped off and mailed to me with a message?"

"Nope, they didn't," she said, sounding suddenly curious. She inched toward Nick, still clutching her robe. "What was the message?"

"The note in the box with his penis said 'Stop the rapes!' Any idea what he was involved in?"

"Nothing would surprise me about that asshole. He tried to rape me when we were kids. Like I said—super-asshole."

"You just referred to his dickhead friend. Who would that be?"

"Terry. Terry LeForte, another real piece of crap," she said, looking down at the cement floor. "They worked together, hung out together, chased women together."

"Rape? Did they rape women together?" Nick asked.

"Not rape. They would meet women at the bar, slip something in their drinks, then take them home."

"So, they drugged women and had sex with them without their consent? That's pretty much classified as rape," Nick said.

"It's not rape if she doesn't resist. Guy and Terry had their fun with them and then took them home. That's not rape, that's a date."

Sandy's response shocked Nick, but he pushed ahead and followed her lead. "Did Guy and Terry have lots of these dates?"

She pointed to two boxes on a shelf in the garage. Guy's name was printed on the side of each. "Picked them up from the landlord in Grand Blanc. One on the left is old bills and paperwork. What's inside the other box tells me those boys had lots of fun and lots of dates."

Without waiting for Sandy's authorization, Nick lifted the box on the right from the shelf and tore off the tape. It was as light as air and was full of women's undergarments. Panties, garter belts, lacy slips—all different sizes and colors. Trophies, Nick thought, the bastards.

The reporter spotted a yellowing copy of the *Saginaw News* next to the bin of overflowing beer bottles and spread it on the cement floor. He poured the contents of the box onto the newspaper and used his cell phone to snap off several photos of the garments, with the box in the picture.

"Did you tell the cops about this box?" Nick asked, moving the garments around on the newspaper with the tip of his pen.

Sandy shook her head no. "They didn't ask."

"You should hold on to this box and its contents," he said. "Probably the other one too. I think they're definitely going to want to analyze them."

Nick asked where Terry lived.

Sandy said she had no idea, other than somewhere in the Flint area. "They worked together—Silverado Soldiers," she said. "Chevy truck plant assembly line."

Chapter 12
Wednesday evening
St. Clementine's Catholic Church

Natalie waited in her vehicle outside St. Clementine's, a Virginia Slim dangling from her lips as she puffed. She used her fingers to stub the butt smoldering in the ashtray. She felt edgy, but lightened when the tall, lanky priest ambled down the sidewalk, stopping to chat briefly with parishioners who were already gathering for confession. She liked how he was casual and friendly with members of his flock.

Natalie counted how many folks had gathered to ask forgiveness for their transgressions. Seven—what appeared to be three couples and a lone grandmother—made their way into the South End church after the priest. Natalie wondered how many stragglers might show up.

But that was it—only the seven. When the first confessors exited the church, she took it as her signal to enter. Natalie wanted to be last in line—no surprises this time. No one popping up just as she was about to spill her guts to the priest.

When the last parishioners had finished, lit their candles in memory of loved ones, and completed their penance, she entered the confessional.

Father Bob slid open the door between them. She could see his lean features through the screen and heard him breathing softly. Same cheap aftershave as the last time. After a moment, he said she could begin.

"Bless me, Father, for I have sinned. It has been two days since my last confession," Natalie began, her palms pressed together and fingers in front of her lips. But the priest recognized her voice and interrupted.

"I'm so glad you are here," he said in a calm and reassuring way. "Have you thought more about your sins since you were here last? Are you truly sorry and remorseful?"

Natalie paused before answering. "I'm not there yet, Father. I thought if I told you what happened, then it might be easier to take the next step. This is driving me crazy. I've got to find a way to get past it."

Father Bob took the unusual step of asking her to remain in place while he looked out into the church to see if anyone else was waiting for him. The building was empty.

"I'm the last one," Natalie said. "I waited to make sure of it. I'm afraid I might have been overheard the last time."

The priest did not respond to the comment. She wondered if he had heard her. He sat back down and asked her to proceed. She thought about repeating the line about being overheard, but decided to come back to it later.

Natalie started with some basic background information to give Father Bob perspective on her life. She described how she had been left alone to take care of her daughters after her loving husband was killed in a firefight in Afghanistan. His death had rocked her family to its foundation, but she'd pushed ahead to give her kids the best life she could.

Natalie had become a licensed Realtor and enjoyed modest success helping people buy and sell property in the Bay City area. The job was ideal; her broker allowed her to keep flexible floor hours—when she was scheduled to be in the office to greet walk-in clients—and of course she could set her own hours for showings.

But the real estate market could be fickle, rolling up and down with the economy. Natalie said she'd entered a slowdown and was eager for a sale. Like others in the business, her earnings were based on commissions—if she didn't sell, her family didn't eat.

"That's when I made the biggest mistake of my life," she said, weeping softly. "I made an appointment to show a vacant house to a client I had not met. He asked me to show him, his wife, and their two kids a charming suburban ranch home that was well within their budget. I hoped they would write an offer. I needed a payday—real bad."

She paused to check if the priest was absorbing her story. He hadn't moved since she began. Father Bob asked her to continue. His voice was soft and welcoming. Obviously, she thought, he was experienced at getting people to open up to him. Part of the job.

"Well, I got to the house early because I hoped it would make a good impression—so much rides on the first look-see. I turned on the lights, opened the blinds, and lit the two-way fireplace for the kitchen and living room," she said, slowing down her narrative. "When I looked up, the buyer was standing in the doorway. I remember thinking he was as big as a tree. He smiled, introduced himself, real friendly. Said his family was on the way in his wife's car.

"That set off alarm bells for me. I suggested we go outside to view the grounds and wait for his family. He saw the small holster on the side of my bag that holds my mace and reached for it the same time I did. He said, 'No, I think we're staying in here.' He twisted the mace out of my hand and sprayed my eyes. I screamed and fell backward. He pushed me down and used a zip tie from his jacket to bind my hands."

The recollection of that moment of horror made her sob and shake. She told Father Bob she'd kicked at her attacker wildly, hoping to wedge a knee between them and push him away. But he was too strong. Then she'd heard the front door slam shut, she said, and a second man had grabbed her ankles. The two men dragged her down a hallway to a main floor bedroom.

"They took turns on me," she screamed through tears and sobs. Natalie covered her eyes with her hands. Her body shook. They'd stripped and beaten her. Biting, pinching, slapping. "I wanted to die. I thought for sure they'd kill me, because at that moment, I believed my life was over and I had entered hell."

Father Bob stepped out of the confessional, opened her door, and helped the trembling Natalie into a pew. The woman fought to regain her composure. She was still shaking. She wanted a cigarette, maybe two. The priest said nothing and sat beside her in the empty church while her shrieks and sobs echoed off the walls.

"My child, there's nothing I can say that will ease your pain," he said in a soft tone. "Nothing can erase the pain you suffered. But you can pray to God and ask for strength and an open heart to heal. I know how you feel. I know your agony."

Natalie sat up straight and looked Father Bob in the eye. "Excuse me, you do not know how I feel. You do not know my agony. I cannot close my eyes at night without seeing and hearing those two animals grunting and slobbering on top of me. You don't know. You can't, so don't try to give me that bullshit."

Father Bob closed his eyes and rocked in the pew silently. After a few moments, he raised his head and spoke. "I know. Believe me, I know. Monsters raped me at seminary. I was fourteen. Over and over again, I was passed around. I cried. I pleaded. I can still see them, I can still hear them. Gross pigs. It went on for two years. They hurt me and I thought I would never get over it."

Natalie stopped crying, watching the priest. "How did you go on? How did you get past it?"

"I'm still not past it," he said. The two held hands as they faced each other in the pew. "I prayed for strength and clarity. I prayed for an open mind and heart. And God gave me the strength to forgive my attackers. That's the only way you can move forward. You can't go on with your heart filled with hate and anger."

Natalie pulled her hands back and stood. "Never. Never. Never." She cleared her throat. "I will never forgive those bastards. They took everything from me and left me like a pile of trash. I watched Larry squeeze the life out of them, and I applauded. The last thing those two creeps saw was my smiling face, and the last thing they heard was my laugh. And then we carved up that scum, mixed it with shit, and spread it on a farm field for burial. After more than a year of pain and agony, revenge was the only thing that let me move on. It was sweet. And now, Father, we have connected with others who have been raped, and we're taking out the vermin."

Father Bob stood too. "If that's true, then why are you still hurting? Why are you still in pain, still crying and shaking? The sweet taste of revenge is always short lived. Forgiveness is for the forgiver, not necessarily the forgiven. It is the only way forward."

The woman scoffed. "God knows what happened to me. I know in my heart He understands what I did and why I did it. God is all-knowing."

"True," Father Bob said, "but you cannot look past number five. Thou shalt not kill. The fifth commandment. The word of God."

Natalie had already thought this through. "The ten commandments are for humans to live by. The men we are killing are subhuman, less than animals, really, in the food chain. Rapists, pedophiles, and kidnappers are deviants whose behavior is so despicable, they forfeit their right to be among us. We are doing humanity a favor by eliminating them."

"My child, my child," Father Bob said, "that is not for you to judge. We are all God's children."

Natalie wheeled around in the pew and stomped toward the church's front door, her heels slapping tile floors and echoing across the cavernous expanse. "Never, Father, never! I will not forget, I will

Murder, so Sweet

not forgive. My job is to send rapists to burn in hell—not forgive them."

The woman disappeared into the night.

Father Bob followed her to the parking lot and shouted, "My door is always open."

Chapter 13
Thursday morning
Flushing

Genesee County tax records indicated that Terry LeForte's last known address was what turned out to be a rundown shack on Pasadena Avenue, located just east of the posh suburb of Flushing. As Nick tooled down the street, he passed one piece-of-crap home after another. Stray dogs roamed the neighborhood. Illegal dumping had turned the area into a continuous trash heap.

An old man, barely able to stand, ambled down the sidewalk. Nick waved at him, and the old guy offered a toothless smile and raised a bottle wrapped in a wrinkled brown paper bag.

Nick stopped the Firebird and lowered his passenger's-side window. "Hiya, pal. Got a minute?"

The old man nodded and stepped toward the vehicle.

"You lived here long? I'm looking for someone from this neighborhood."

"Yup, moved here twenty years ago. Had all my kids on this street," he said, swinging the bottled hand over his head at houses on both sides of Pasadena, "and some of them had the same mamma."

The reporter smiled. "You know a guy named Terry LeForte? I hear he was a ladies' man too. He may have a winning lottery ticket he hasn't cashed in yet."

The old man rubbed the gray stubble under his chin. He looked Nick up and down and scanned the inside of the Firebird. "Ain't seen him in ages. He used to live at the end of the block. Rented from a guy named Robinson who owns a shitload of property on this street."

"Is Mr. Robinson still around? Would like to bend his ear a bit."

The old guy took a swig from his bottle. A stream of liquid splashed through the stubble onto his open flannel shirt. He tossed the empty bottle into the overgrown weeds of a lot with a burned-out house on it. "Call him Robbie, everyone does. That's him putting a railin' on the front porch down there."

Nick spotted the guy working on the porch and thanked Gray Whiskers for his help.

"Yup, but Terry wasn't no ladies' man. No, sir-ee," the old guy said, swaying slightly. "You ain't no ladies' man if you got to use force. You just a brute, and he was nasty and mean to the women he and his buddy brought onto this street. Real ugly. Lots of cryin' and screamin' late at night."

Nick nodded and opened his glove box. He handed Gray Whiskers a silver flask. The guy grabbed it like he was greeting an old friend, flicked open the top, and took a long pull on the flask before returning it to Nick.

He wiped his lips on his shirt sleeve. "Thanks, my man. That's got some kick to it."

As Nick pulled away, he watched Gray Whiskers wobble, then sit down on the broken sidewalk. It was a quarter after nine in the morning, and the old guy was well on his way to a numbing buzz. The reporter looked for Robbie, who was wrestling with a long two-by-four chunk of lumber with one hand while wielding a power tool with his other.

Nick hopped out of his parked hot rod and offered Robbie a hand. "Let me hold the end while you screw it to that post."

"Hold it up a little higher," Robbie said, checking Nick out as they worked on the railing. The power tool did its job with a couple quick zips. "What you want?"

Nick used his chin to point out the man now stretched out prone on the sidewalk. "I hear a guy I'm looking for rents from you. Name's Terry LeForte. He still on this street?"

"Nope, not no more," Robbie said, setting his power drill on the ground. "You a cop?"

Nick moved closer. "I'm a reporter from Bay City. Looking into the deaths of a couple of guys. One of them might be LeForte. I found an address on this street from tax records."

"He been gone for quite a while, a year or so at least. Just up and disappeared. Still owes me three months' rent. Had a buddy help me clean out his place. We put his shit on the street, and the neighbors picked it clean."

Nick asked if anyone else in the neighborhood might know what had become of LeForte. Robbie said the man had one close friend in the area. At one point, they'd lived together on Pasadena. The landlord jotted down an address for Nick but said he wasn't sure if LeForte's friend would still be there.

"You're free to knock on doors to see who remembers him," Robbie said with a smile. "But keep in mind, most folks in this neighborhood answer their doors with a pistol or shotgun. Don't say I didn't warn you."

Nick jumped back into his sweet ride and rolled farther down Pasadena to the address the landlord had provided. The place was a wreck, but he could see movement through a few of the windows that had not been shot out. He thought about the warning he'd been given, and decided to knock on the door anyway. He'd come too far to turn back without at least trying.

No answer, and no more movement inside the place. Nick checked the side door. It had been nailed shut, probably as a security measure after the deadbolt lock was busted out by a battering ram during a police raid.

Still no answer. Nick decided against trying the door at the rear of the house—it was guarded by a pit bull that strained the links of a ten-foot chain. The mangled mutt yapped and howled at Nick like the reporter had a string of sausage tied around his neck.

When Nick returned to his vehicle, he discovered two men checking it out. His keys were in his pants pocket. He wondered if he would have to fight his way off Pasadena Avenue.

"Hey, guys, what's up?" he asked. The two pulled back from the Firebird as Nick approached. "I've had her for about twenty years."

"Just admiring your ride, man," said the larger of the two. Both looked to be in their late twenties. They were dressed in mismatched sweats and scuffed-up tennis shoes. Their empty hands were in clear view. Nick figured they lived nearby. No other vehicles were in the street. "Don't see many purdy cars with big V-8s in 'em on this street. That got a 350 in it? You a salesman?"

Nick relaxed slightly. "It's a 396, fuel injected with an overhead cam. And nope, I'm a newspaper guy just looking for someone who has gone missing. Either of you know Terry LeForte?"

The men glanced at each other, and the bigger man pointed to the house Nick had just visited. "Terry's cousin lives there. He might know something. Hold on. I'll get him for you."

After thirty seconds of fist-pounding against the front door, it opened a crack. "What the hell do you want?" asked a raspy, irritated voice from inside the dump. "I'm not buying nothin'."

"A.J., get your ass out here. Got a man wants to talk to you."

"Tell him to go away."

The bigger man yanked open the door and grabbed A.J. by his shirt collar, pulling him out onto the porch. The first thing Nick noticed was his bright-red hair, too bright to not come out of a box. He was razor-blade skinny, with dirty work pants, a torn T-shirt, and angry eyes. Open sores on his arms seeped.

"Damn it. That hurt," he said, squaring off with the big man. "Told you, got nothin' to say."

A.J. moved back toward the door. Nick played his ace in the hole, a line of crap about money. "I'm here because I figured you'd want to know that your cousin Terry is dead. The state may owe him two years of overpaid taxes. You might be able to collect. You just have to file for it."

"Say what?" A.J. exclaimed, giving the reporter his undivided attention. "How much we talkin' about?"

A minute ago, Skinny Red wouldn't come out of his shithole. Now he was ready to cash in from a cousin he hadn't seen or heard from in more than a year.

Nick pressed forward with his line of bullshit, which he didn't mind spreading if it led to information about Terry. "Not sure. It could be a tidy little sum. Before you can get to the money to find out, though, Terry's remains must be identified and his death verified."

Skinny Red checked the faces of each man in front of him. He nodded at Nick. "What we gotta do to figure it out?"

"DNA. I need his DNA to see if it matches what was found. Can you help me get DNA samples?"

"Where in the hell would we find it? He lived here only six months before he just up and went off somewhere." A.J. gestured with his right hand. "Figured he was out partying some place, maybe Florida, with his buddy, Guy."

Nick told him that Terry's DNA might be found in his personal effects. Did his cousin have a comb in the house, or a razor or toothbrush? Anything that might have his skin cells on it? Something in a medicine cabinet?

A.J. wiped his nose and dug at a mole on his chin while he

thought. "Hold on a minute," he said, "got an idea." He ducked into the shack. From the porch, Nick peered inside. Dark, dusty, cramped. Probably smelly. A hoarder's haven. Old newspapers and magazines were piled to the ceiling, with trash everywhere. Multiple dog turds lay in a corner. The reporter decided he would wait outside.

After several minutes of clanking—junk being tossed around, Nick thought—Skinny Red emerged with a small bag. He held it up as if it were some kind of grand prize. "Well, lookie here. Hit the jackpot," he said.

It was a beat-up and filthy shaving kit. Nick pulled on the zipper and spotted two straight razors, a comb with half its teeth missing, a toothbrush that looked like it had been used to shine shoes, and at least two used condoms—or old plastic gloves. Terry's name was scrawled on the bag's inside flap.

Nick took photos of the bag and what he could see of its contents. He was especially careful not to mess with the plastic—whether gloves or condoms, it could be helpful.

As he turned the bag over, he felt an object just below the zipper of a side pocket. Inside, Nick discovered a memory card. Could be photos, maybe video, he thought, and placed the card back in the bag. Officer Quinn could check out the bag and its contents when they were turned in.

"Jackpot might be exactly the right word," Nick said. He went to the trunk of his Firebird and pulled out a large plastic storage bag. "Stick the whole thing in here. This might lead you to a pot of gold."

The reporter jumped back into his hot rod and fired it up. The two guys who had been admiring the vehicle asked him to make the engine bark. Nick hit the gas pedal and the big V-8 growled, revving deep and hard.

"Smoke them tires," the bigger man pleaded.

Nick was happy to oblige. He burned rubber from both rear wheels between driveways on Pasadena. That turned the guys into teenagers, whooping and hollering at the sound of an old-fashioned American muscle car. The commotion and smoke even prompted Gray Whiskers to look up from his prone position on the sidewalk. He grinned and waved at Nick as the reporter drove past.

Nick's cell phone pinged. It was a text from J.R. Ratchett: "Got another body out here. All chopped up into bits. Discovered by some kids. This is getting bad, real bad."

Nick alerted the newsroom and pointed the Firebird toward Bay City.

Chapter 14
Thursday noon
Bay City, West Side

Natalie O'Brien waited patiently in the parking lot of the Lindenhoff Restaurant on Euclid Avenue. She'd shown up early for the monthly meeting of the Bay City Noon Optimists Club because she hoped to identify the woman she thought she recognized from confession at St. Clementine's Catholic Church.

Natalie knew many of the members professionally and personally. She enjoyed the positive, uplifting attitude of the club, and it had become an important and vital civic organization for her as a licensed Realtor. Club meetings were perfect for networking. She did not want the dynamic surrounding the club to change because one of its members had become too nosy, listening in on her private confession. Another good reason for Natalie to find out the identity of the woman from St. Clementine's and deal with her if necessary.

Just before noon, Natalie spotted the antique yellow Cadillac rolling into the parking lot. The Caddy was so big, it looked like a tank painted the color of a banana. When the massive hunk of steel settled to a stop, it swallowed up two full parking spaces. Natalie was positive it was the vehicle of the woman she'd seen after confession Monday night.

The driver's side door opened, and sure enough, out stepped the short, stout woman with silver-blond curls and black earmuffs. Natalie slid out of her van and followed Earmuff Lady into the restaurant, careful to keep her distance. At the registration desk, the woman chatted briefly with the greeter, who was secretary-treasurer of the organization, before signing in for the meeting.

When Natalie's turn came to sign in, she jotted her name right beneath the signature of Andrea Pilinski, who was standing nearby and talking with another Optimist. Natalie noted Andrea's name, typed it into her cell phone contacts, and proceeded as if this were just another meeting.

Earmuff Lady had been identified. Natalie would decide later if the woman in the yellow Caddy was a real threat to her and her siblings, and how to deal with her. She sent text messages to Kate and Larry: "Let's get together for wine after kids in bed."

When Natalie believed no one was watching, she slipped out the restaurant's side door. In her mind, there was no need to stick around. She had a name for the woman who was keeping her awake at night. Time to go.

Andrea Pilinski steered her Cadillac, which had been Ralph's pride and joy, into the two parking spaces that the Bay City Noon Optimists Club had saved for her in the lot outside the Lindenhoff Restaurant on Euclid Avenue.

The monthly meetings were a treat for Andrea. She had been an active member of the club since her daughters were small. She loved the club's emphasis on youngsters, with the stated goal "to make the future brighter by bringing out the best in children, in their communities, and in themselves." Today the Polish grandmother hoped to get authorization for an idea she had for a children's program.

Andrea entered the restaurant and was immediately greeted by "Well, hello, sunshine!" Rene Jones, the secretary-treasurer, was dressed in powder blue from head to toe; her arms were stretched wide for a hug. The two women docked like jetliners gliding into airport terminals. They patted each other on the back as if they were old friends who had drifted apart.

"So glad to see you, Andrea," Rene said. "We should get together more often than these monthly meetings. Let's start planning for midmonth luncheons to catch up."

Andrea thought the idea was splendid. "Love to. Let me get signed in, and then I'd like to chat with you about the party at the mission."

She pulled off her hat and her earmuffs, allowing her silver-blond curls to bounce like they'd been freed from a corral. Andrea signed her name on the registration sheet and looked for the coat rack. As she did, Rene greeted another member: "Well, hello, sunshine. So good to see you again."

Andrea turned back toward Rene as a third member signed in. "I wanted to ask you about the monthly birthday party program for children living at the Good Samaritan Rescue Mission. I think our club should buy small gifts for the kids and sponsor a party with games, crafts, and, of course, birthday cake, don't you know."

"Fabulous idea," Rene said. "What a wonderful thing to do for young people who have had such a hard time of it. The Mission is a godsend, but life there can be difficult for little ones. I don't think it would cost the club that much either."

Delighted, Andrea made a note of it in her planner. As she closed the book, she heard Rene speak with another member, asking how the real estate market was faring.

The member replied that the market was strong and getting better. "Earlier, I thought it was going to hell, but not now. You know me, I'm always optimistic."

That voice struck a chord with Andrea, particularly when the H-double-hockey-sticks word was used. A chill ran through her body. Andrea knew the voice belonged to the woman from the St. Clementine's confessional. Was a cold-blooded murderer standing nearby? How could a murderer be an Optimist? She thought. Murder was so very negative.

She didn't turn to see where the voice came from. Instead she remained motionless, waiting to hear more. When the woman spoke again, Andrea knew she was the one from the confessional—no doubt about it.

After the other club members took their seats, Andrea doubled back to Registration and checked the sign-in sheet. Two lines under her name was "Natalie O'Brien." Confessor identified. Murderer pinpointed, at least in her mind.

Now she had to figure out what to do with the information.

Reporting to police what she thought she'd overheard in confession might thrust her into the *Looney Toons* category, she feared. Andrea's family on her mother's side had a history of mental illness. And she'd watched Ralph slowly descend into the darkness of dementia. It wasn't pretty to watch, and she'd heard the hurtful words of friends and relatives who spoke quietly about Ralph losing his mind. She knew that when elderly people started to slip, whispers began about dementia and Alzheimer's.

With the unexpected discovery of the mystery confessor, Andrea struggled to stay tuned into the Optimists meeting. It wasn't important anymore—not with murder on the line.

Chapter 15
Thursday afternoon
Bay City Blade newsroom

By the time Nick returned to the newsroom, Dave's fingers were clacking away on his keyboard about the new body that had turned up in the Thumb. Dave had interviewed the Huron County sheriff, the commander of the state police forensic science lab, and the superintendent of Caseville Schools.

Chaos reigned in Caseville, where the body was discovered early that morning, Dave said. Nick started writing an insert for Dave's article. It included new information about Guy Devereaux and Terry LeForte.

The reporters flipped through their notes as they talked about the news report that would soon be published. They agreed it was another strong package that would inform readers throughout the region but also advance the story.

A MOREL TO THE STORY
Students hunt for tasty mushroom; make ghastly discovery in woods

By Dave Balz and Nick Steele, *Blade* **reporters**

Education took on new meaning this morning for a group of Caseville seventh-grade students who were scheduled to hunt for morel mushrooms at the Sand Point Nature Preserve, but instead discovered the grisly remains of what appeared to be more human tissue spread just inside the preserve's entrance to the woods.

83

The Huron County sheriff said grief counselors tried to comfort traumatized students today as parents were called to pick up their children. Investigators said they are combing the crime scene, which includes the parking lot and the walkway leading into the woods of the two-hundred-acre preserve located five miles west of Caseville at the base of Wild Fowl Bay.

The horrific scene unfolded this morning when Donna Gentry's science class arrived with bag lunches at the preserve. Bright sunshine and warm spring air greeted twenty-three seventh-graders, according to their teacher, who supervises the annual field trip to hunt for morel mushrooms. A few days of warm weather made morels pop out of the ground like tiny soldiers standing at attention—especially around elm, hickory, ash, and sycamore trees in sandy soil.

But soon after students entered the woods, they came out running and screaming, Gentry said. Instead of morels, they found turkey vultures, bald eagles, hawks, and foxes feeding on human remains.

"It was horrifying," said the teacher, who cried while recalling what happened. "This was supposed to be a fun day for students engaging with nature and science after a long, hard winter. But it turned into a nightmare. Can you imagine watching an eagle swoop down and snatch up body parts in its talons? Some of the students tried telling the others what they saw was a deer carcass, but I could tell most didn't believe it."

Deputy J. R. Ratchett was the first to respond to the 911 call. He said the remains were spread in a wide arc on top of the marshy ground—no attempt was made to bury them.

"Looked like a hasty dump," Ratchett said. "I picked up

a handful of remains to check 'em out. Ice cold, even a little frozen. Had to have come out of a fridge or freezer. Probably dumped early this morning or last night.

"We're checking with property owners near the preserve to see what they might have seen or heard. We're not used to this kind of thing, and now we've had body parts turn up in two different areas about twenty-five miles apart."

On Monday, the remains of two men were discovered in a farm field near Pigeon when a farmer began tilling what had been a sugar beet field, authorities said. A fingerprint from a piece of a thumb identified one victim as Guy Devereaux of Grand Blanc. A second victim has been tentatively identified as one of Devereaux's friends. Police are awaiting DNA analysis to confirm the friend as the second victim.

Neighbors and friends of the pair told the *Blade* this morning that both men had worked at the Chevy truck plant on Van Slyke in Flint. They said the two were inseparable friends and had disappeared more than a year ago. No one knew where they went, or cared, for that matter.

After the remains were discovered Monday, two body parts and a note were delivered to the *Blade*. The note said "Stop the rapes." Police are still trying to find out who sent the package to the newspaper.

It is unknown at this point, police said, whether the remains of the two men found near Pigeon are connected to the remains discovered near Sand Point this morning.

Sheriff Donaldson said he still believes the killings are the result of mob hits or gang activity. He does not think the killings could be the work of local residents.

"I can't imagine anyone from our communities being

> capable of such savagery," he said during a telephone interview this morning. "These are revenge murders. Somebody wanted to get back at these victims in the worst way."
>
> Ratchett said he believes the murders must be connected.
>
> "That, or we got a copycat at work," the deputy said. "But I'm not buying the copycat theory, and I don't believe in coincidences. It's too much of a nasty mess to chop up bodies like that. We got us some real sickos at work."
>
> Authorities scoured the entrance of the preserve for fresh tire and foot impressions, but the soggy, marshy soil did not hold imprints well. Additionally, the entrance was open to the public and saw regular traffic—everything from young lovers to partying teens to birdwatchers in search of their feathered friends. Investigators at the scene searched for other forensic evidence, including trash discarded by visitors.
>
> Police urge members of the public to come forward with any possibly relevant information.

Right after final deadline for the first afternoon pressrun, the C-Man called a meeting on the Thumb deaths. He wanted a full update—regardless of what had been published. He also wanted to plan coverage through the weekend.

"Dave, get the photo and graphics people to join the meeting," he said. "We need a full-court press on this story."

When the group had assembled, Clapper told Nick that the Madonna package, originally scheduled to publish Sunday, had now been postponed due to the developing news around the human tissue discovered in the Thumb. Word about the Madonna package being held up again delighted Nick. He still wasn't finished with his part of the story, and he knew that the delay would irritate the hell out of the features editor, whom Nick loved to see tormented—just for the fun of it.

Nick wondered aloud if more bodies would be discovered before Sunday. It was only Thursday afternoon, just a few days after the first tissue was discovered. For now, he wanted to continue chasing the Devereaux/LeForte connection to the crime. The big questions: Were they rapists, and did those penis tips delivered to the *Blade* with a note belong to them? And how were they related to the body tissue discovered today?

Dave hoped to find out more about Andrea Pilinski's tip. The South End woman, he said, had come forward with a fantastic story about overhearing a Catholic confession of murder. But was she reliable? And how was her story connected to what was found in the Thumb?

"She seemed solid to me, but I'd like to check her out more thoroughly," he said. "I talked to her neighbors, the Andersons, who backed up her story regarding the Monday night confession. They say they remember a stranger in the church, but they did not overhear anything. She's active in the community. If I talk to enough people, I should be able to see whether she checks out or goes into the psychic reader and space alien categories."

The chief also suggested that Nick and Dave try to interview the priest. "Yeah, yeah, I know. He's sworn to secrecy of the confessional. But go talk to him. Poke and prod him some and try to gauge his reaction to your questions. You may be able to learn something from what he doesn't say and how he doesn't say it."

Nick was about to suggest that he and Dave double-team on interviews with Andrea Pilinski and Father Bob, when the conference room door swung open and a pressman placed a small box on the table. Nick's name was printed on it in black felt marker.

"Found this by the back door when I went out to smoke—figured you would want to know right away," said Bill, whose coveralls were smudged with black ink. "By the way, guys in the pressroom think you should tell the public what kind of body parts were delivered here. That'd add some spice to your story. Just our thoughts."

The guys in the pressroom, no strangers to the screaming headlines of supermarket tabloids, knew what kind of juicy details turned a good story into one that was absolutely devoured by a dirt-loving public.

The C-Man thanked Bill for delivering the package. "Tell the guys I agree with them," the newsroom chief said, "but we're trying to make the cops happy by holding back what only the killer would know."

The package looked identical to the one left at the *Blade* earlier in the week. When Bill had closed the door, Nick peered inside the box. Contents? What appeared to be one small penis tip and a slip of paper resting at the bottom. The reporter gently lifted the slip of paper out by balancing it on his ink pen. When it reached eye level, Nick read aloud: "Stop the rapes or the bodies will keep showing up in pieces."

The C-Man asked Dave to call the police and suggested everyone in the room stay until the cops arrived. He himself called the *Blade* attorneys. The case had become deadlier, and the contents of the box indicated the body count was about to rise.

Chapter 16
Thursday evening
Natalie O'Brien's home

Three bottles of wine waited on Natalie's dining room table by six o'clock. She wanted to make sure plenty of hooch was available. Tonight's was an important meeting—much to discuss.

Natalie had decided to tell her brother and sister about her visits to Father Bob, and she was afraid it would not be well received. Larry wanted to discuss the issue of body disposal, which had proven difficult with the latest dump of human tissue.

Kate and Larry arrived at nearly the same time, pulling into the driveway at a quarter past six. They entered Natalie's home upbeat and full of energy, teasing each other as they hunted for Natalie's daughters to bid them a good night. When they saw the chilled wine on the table, the festive atmosphere kicked up another notch.

Kate popped open two with a corkscrew, and Larry poured full glasses. The two clinked glasses and gulped down several mouthfuls before Natalie joined them. Their sister offered a salute to the others and slugged down some Chardonnay herself.

Natalie suggested they start the meeting with a recap of their most recent execution. It had gone well until the end. What happened?

Larry tried to explain the complexities of body disposal—particularly when unforeseen circumstances arose. "I didn't account for unseasonably warm weather. And the windmill-powered freezer didn't freeze the bags solid. They were melting the minute I pulled them out.

"Then I got pulled over by a deputy because I had a brake light out, which scared the hell out of me. But no worries. His name was

Booger, and he was a good ol' boy. That delay caused more thawing and threw the target dump site into question. I was being chased by hungry dogs in Bay Port, and it was getting dark. I had to move fast. Kate came up with the new site."

Natalie looked at Kate, incredulous. "So you're the one who thought it would be a good idea to dump a chopped-up body in the path of grade-school kids? And Larry gets pulled over with melting body pieces in the back? And then gets chased by hungry dogs? Did anybody see the dogs chasing you?"

Larry took a double gulp from his glass. "Well, it was the middle of Bay Port. Everybody is either in the bar or sleeping it off. Might have been a couple of grannies coming out of the post office. They pointed and stared."

Now it was Kate's turn to be dumbfounded. "You didn't tell me about witnesses. How long will it take them to call the tip line after they read about what was discovered at the preserve this morning? Get rid of the van, Larry. Make it vanish."

Larry hit his wine glass again. "Okay, I got a guy who can take care of the van. I will ditch it tomorrow. Hey, I did the best I could. I was not going to take that body back to the farm or bring him to Bay City. We gotta have a better system if we're going to continue."

Uncomfortable silence fell over the dining room. The siblings squirmed, peering into their wine glasses. They stole side glances at each other like they needed some kind of affirmation that things were going to be all right.

Finally Natalie spoke, barely above a whisper. "You know, I can't believe we aren't all in chains and locked up in some dungeon awaiting trial right now. What a bunch of screw-ups!"

Kate stood up from her chair and reached across the table to hug her sister. She snagged Larry's shirtsleeve and pulled him into their impromptu squeeze zone. Kate was the chief, the ringleader in the family. She was the one who had gone ballistic when she learned of Natalie's rape and torture. It was Kate who'd called Larry and demanded that the siblings go on the offensive, hunt down the rapists, and kill them.

"I got us in this mess, and I'll get us out," Kate said. Her words had a hard edge, and she stuck her chin out as she issued them. "Nobody's caught us yet. They got nothing on us."

Natalie pulled free from the triangle hug and cleared her throat. She faced her siblings and said she needed to tell them something she had done without their knowledge—or consent. And now she feared it might lead to their downfall.

Kate and Larry refilled their wine glasses. They took long swigs and stared blankly at Natalie. She was their baby sister. She had a long history of doing what she wanted, when she wanted to—without checking with her older siblings, who were often left cleaning up the mess. That was Natalie's style. Sometimes she was a one-person high-wire act while the rest of the family watched, holding their collective breath.

Larry broke the silence. "Okay, so what did you do? 'Fess up."

Natalie blurted out a laugh. "Well, that's what I did. I confessed to a priest. Father Bob. Nice guy."

If Kate's sternum hadn't been in the way, her jaw would have hit the floor. "You what? No, no, no. We pledged to each other that we would tell no one. And now you say you blabbed to a priest. I can't believe this."

Larry shared Kate's outrage. "You're not even a good Catholic. You're like borderline, when convenient, when it suits your needs, Catholic. Why suddenly need a priest's forgiveness for something we all agreed had to be done? I'm surprised you remembered the confessional ritual, it's been that long. Seriously, why?"

Larry and Kate were mortified—little sis had done it again. Once more, she'd taken them all to the edge of the cliff, and they wobbled while they looked over the edge. Would this be the time when Natalie's impulsivity would cause them to fall to their demise?

Natalie refilled her glass. She explained that she felt confession was something she had to do—even if it didn't result in absolution. Revenge was delightful, but not enough.

"Larry, when you squeezed the life out of those two dirtbags as they looked me in the eye, I absolutely loved that," Natalie said, noting the experience was better than sex. Truly orgasmic, she continued, the most thrilling moment of her life. "But the moment passed," she said. "It wasn't enough. It didn't fix me."

Natalie insisted that she'd made a connection with Father Bob, and she hoped he would help her. "The priest is my soul mate," she said, lighting a cigarette. "He understands what happened to me because it happened to him too. He knows the humiliation, the degradation, the dehumanization that rape causes. We totally connected."

More silence as this latest fact—the priest had experienced rape—sank in with Larry and Kate. Each of the O'Briens drained their glasses. Natalie jabbed out her smoke and slipped away to check on her daughters. Her absence gave her siblings a chance to talk.

Kate grabbed Larry's arm. "Natalie has stepped over the edge if she thinks a priest is her soul mate. Does she think she's going to get the priest to agree with her and say, 'Yup, killing those bad dudes was okay'?"

Larry nodded in agreement. "She's getting wacky. Desperate to heal from the rape and trying to justify the revenge killing. Maybe it's all too much for her."

When Natalie returned, she indicated there was one more thing to discuss.

"Kids nodded off, they're all good," she said, failing to make eye contact with Larry and Kate. "But I should also mention another tiny, little problem that may or may not be a problem at all. And it's one I will take care of."

The pronouncement caught Larry and Kate by surprise. What now? How could there be more? How could it be worse?

"Spill," Kate said, spitting the word out as if it tasted like vinegar. "What else?"

Natalie busied herself collecting the empty wine bottles. Only one bottle remained, and her siblings were eyeballing its contents.

"No worries. I found and identified the woman who I think overheard my confession," she said, pushing the words out as quickly as possible as if that would lessen their impact. "She's a little old Polish lady who has silver-blond curls and a pink face."

The statement floored Larry and Kate.

"Ho-ly shit," Larry barked. "Somebody heard you confess to two murders? We are all going to prison. This will be the end of us."

Kate wanted to know how she'd identified the woman if she was in the opposite confessional. "How do you know she heard anything, and how could you know who she is?"

"Well, my confession got a little loud, and I didn't know she was in the opposite confessional until I heard the door click shut. She had to have heard me. Anyway, I waited for her to come out of the church. I recognized her from Noon Optimists. Saw her come into the meeting today."

Kate and Larry looked at each other in disbelief. It had been an evening of shocking admissions and disheartening screw-ups. But it was about to go in a whole new direction.

"Stop fretting," Natalie said, pouring the last of the wine into her siblings' outstretched glasses. "If I think she's a threat to us, then I'll just take her out, and we move on."

The bottoms of the tumblers went straight up in the air. When

Kate and Larry finished their glasses, they grunted and wiped their lips.

Larry jumped in first. "No, absolutely not. I agreed to kill and get rid of the bodies of the scum who attacked and hurt you. I am not having anything to do with killing a little old Polish lady from the South End. No way. We kill rapists. That's the code we pledged to. She falls outside of the code. Count me out."

Kate agreed. "Too far, Natalie. We're not going there. You are off the rails. Killing a little old grandmother—that's not us."

Natalie smiled and lit a smoke. "Don't worry. I got this."

Chapter 17
Friday morning
Dixie Highway, Flint

At precisely six o'clock, the big steel double gate at the entrance to Rest in Pieces Used Auto Parts opened with a screech. Larry O'Brien inched his van through the entryway and pulled inside an outbuilding near the main office of the giant junkyard.

It was one of more than a half-dozen mega vehicle salvage yards that lined Dort Highway on the north end of Flint. They were home to thousands of wrecks and junkers waiting to be parted out or scrapped for recycling. But R.I.P. was also the kind of place where five hundred bucks placed in the right hands could result in the quick disappearance of a vehicle altogether.

Larry had served in Iraq during Operation Desert Storm with the owner of R.I.P's son, Jeb, who was considered the battalion scavenger—the guy who could procure just about anything. Need a Jeep? A helicopter? Anti-aircraft artillery? Call Jeb—if he couldn't get it, nobody could. Jeb and Larry made a heck of a team. Jeb could find anything under the sun and Larry was a well-known fixer, the Ray Donovan of Baghdad. Larry knew how to work in the shadows and make connections within the military and local government. He knew how to grant a favor to a friend—with the understanding that the favor would one day be returned.

After Larry was spanked by Kate and Natalie Thursday night for the clumsy disposal of their latest victim, he called his old army buddy, using his burner cell phone. Said he had a delicate problem with a vehicle and asked if Jeb could help him take care of it. Jeb told him to be at the front gate at six in the morning and to bring donuts—jelly and cream filled.

95

Larry left Bay City just after four thirty, snaking south down back roads through Frankenmuth and Birch Run. He watched his speed, used his turn signals, and was careful not to make any rolling stops. Though his brake lights had been fixed, he double-checked to make sure they worked without flaw. His only stop was for fresh baked goods. Larry didn't relax until the gate at R.I.P. creaked open.

Once inside the massive junkyard, he parked in the three-sided outbuilding. There the van's gasoline tank was punctured, letting the fluid flow into an open pit. Same thing with the radiator, engine oil, and transmission reservoirs. The van's license plate disappeared and its VIN was chipped off. Now it was an empty, hapless van with no owner and no history.

While the van drained, the old friends scarfed the pastry, washing it down with coffee that looked like dirty dishwater.

"I'm smart enough to know not to ask why you want to ditch the van, but why in hell do you want to ditch the van?" Jeb asked between bites of a gooey cherry turnover. "Looks like she's still in good shape."

"Well, don't look too hard," Larry replied, avoiding direct eye contact. "If you pulled up the carpet in the back, you'd get a view we saw all too often in Baghdad. I need that—and the whole vehicle—to disappear."

"Figured it was something bad by the sound of your voice on the phone." Jeb pulled a small round container out of his hip pocket, removed a gob of tobacco, and stuck it into his mouth between cheek and gum. "Want a pinch?"

Larry declined the offer, declaring he had quit when he returned to the states. "All I can say is, this is a sticky situation and I can't let that van get discovered by cops."

Jeb nodded. "I got your back, buddy. It will be gone before you get past the city limits." The two men shook hands.

Murder, so Sweet

A four-wheel drive John Deere with a front-end loader appeared out of nowhere, chugging from behind a stack of junk pickup trucks. It dragged the van to the other side of the yard and fed it to Big Papa—the boneyard's monster crusher. The giant compactor's engine roared, ready to cook Big Papa breakfast. When Jeb pushed the button on the crusher's portable control, a steel plate, driven by high-powered hydraulics, methodically descended until it flattened the van like an elephant stepping on a soda can.

When Big Papa's steel plate rose again, the John Deere snagged the crushed hunk of junk and loaded it onto a flatbed truck. Three more wrecks were flattened by Big Papa and ended up on top of Larry's flapjack van. The load was secured, and Larry watched the flatbed head south on Dixie Highway for one of metro Detroit's biggest recycling yards.

As Larry shook Jeb's hand again, he pulled an envelope half as fat as a brick from his inside breast pocket. "Thanks, buddy. I know I can always count on a Ranger. I'll sleep better tonight."

"You need a ride?"

"Nope, my sister will be pulling up to your front gate any minute. I'm gonna go wait for her. Thanks again."

By nine o'clock, Larry was back in Bay City. He called 911 and reported that his van had been stolen from his driveway overnight—discovered it when he went outside to go to work. When he hung up, he sighed, the knots in his neck finally letting go.

At nine thirty that same morning, Father Bob left the room of one of his parishioners at Bay Medical Center and checked his watch. When he looked up, Nick Steele and Dave Balz stood smiling in his path.

Nick spoke first, reaching for a handshake. "Father Bob, I'm Nick Steele from the *Blade*, and this is my associate, Dave Balz. Know you're busy, but wondered if we could get a quick word with you?"

The reporter didn't let go of his hand, and Dave positioned his squat, stocky body to cut off any attempt by the priest to flee. Father Bob opened his mouth, but no words came out. His gaze darted between the two reporters.

"It won't take long," Nick continued, not letting go. "We can slip into the chapel down the hall. Nobody is using it right now. Dave checked."

The priest glanced at his watch again. "Sick people are waiting for me. I make these rounds on schedule. I can't disappoint."

"We know," Nick said. "We checked with the woman in your office. She told us right where you'd be in your rounds. This won't take but a few minutes, and then we'll get out of your hair."

The reporter started moving toward the chapel, tugging the priest along with him. Dave scooted ahead and opened the chapel door. The room was dimly lit, with two beautiful stained-glass images of angels amid fluffy clouds. Spotlights behind the glass magnified the peaceful effect. Fresh flowers and lit candles gave the room a welcoming, comfortable feel. Soft chairs sat on one side of the room, and kneelers awaited those who wanted to pray or meditate.

"What can I help you with?" Father Bob asked, using his left hand to free his right from Nick's grip. He glanced between the reporters once more. "I must say, this is highly unusual."

Dave sat in one of the chairs and motioned for Father Bob to take a seat. "Father, we're here because of a report from a member of your flock—actually, it may involve two members."

Nick blocked the door in case the priest decided to bolt.

Father Bob raised his right hand like a stop sign. "I really can't discuss the private discussions I have with parishioners. It would be inappropriate."

Nick jumped into the conversation. "We're talking murder, Father. No sin bigger than that. This is important because we believe others may be at risk. That's why we're here."

Father Bob smiled and visibly relaxed. "Now, you're both smart guys. You know I can't reveal anything that is talked about in confession. Either of you Catholic? You know how it works, right?"

Dave shook his head no. "We're not Catholic, but we are aware of your restrictions. We were told that a conversation you had about the murders came outside of the confessional. I interviewed Andrea Pilinski. She called us because she was so upset by what she heard inside your church. I spent quite a bit of time with her. She seemed genuine and sincere—I never had the feeling I was talking to a fruitcake."

The priest looked down at the floor, then checked his watch a third time. "Our discussion was private. I consider it confidential, and I don't want to comment on what was said specifically, but I will tell you this: Andrea, sweet and delightful as she may seem on the outside, is a troubled woman. Simply not the same since she lost Ralph to dementia. She hears voices. And I'll tell you what I told her. You can't trust anything you think you might overhear from the confessional. What's said in confession is usually whispered conversation. Even if you try to listen real hard, it sounds like mumbling. Nothing that could be used in court, and certainly nothing that should be read in a newspaper article."

The priest's assertion made Dave do a double-take. He hadn't gotten that read on Andrea at all. "I will check with others who know her and see if they feel the same way as you," he said.

Nick decided to try another run at Father Bob to see if he would reveal more, whether on purpose or by accident. "So, what you're acknowledging to us is that Andrea really did overhear a confession at St. Clementine's, but you're suggesting she merely misunderstood what was said. Is that correct?"

Father Bob grimaced and stood up. Nick had hit a nerve. "I'm not acknowledging or suggesting anything. I'm telling you I can't discuss any of this, and I'm simply urging you to be wary of what you hear from Andrea. She's getting older and can't remember things from one day to the next. Now, I must go. More sick folks to tend to."

Nick stepped aside from the doorway. "Thanks, Father, we appreciate your time. But I know you read the newspaper. Dave and I are hanging all over these murders like a rolling summer storm. We're not going away, and we may come back to talk with you again."

The priest smiled pleasantly and moved toward the open door. "I've said all I'm going to say to you or the police. I won't discuss this again."

When Father Bob left the chapel, Nick reached into his jacket breast pocket and clicked off the recorder. "Well, that was interesting. We got a lot more than I expected."

Dave nodded in agreement. "We now know for a fact that Andrea overheard a confession last Monday night—just need to find out if she's off her rocker."

At eleven o'clock, J.R. Ratchett placed a call to Nick Steele. The deputy had exciting news to share with the reporter—a new lead in the Thumb body tissue murders.

Nick, who had returned to the *Blade* after interviewing the priest from St. Clementine's, took the call without hesitation. "Hey, deputy, what's up? Glad to hear we've got a break in the case."

Ratchett was so excited, he could hardly get the words out. He said he'd received word from the sheriff's tip hotline that two women in Bay Port had reported an unusual scene in front of the post office Wednesday on Promenade Street, the village's main drag.

"Nick, get this, they claim they saw an old van drive through town with a whole bunch of dogs chasing it," he said, his voice breaking. "So, what would have been in the back of that van that would drive dogs crazy? Made me wonder if he was carrying the body parts that showed up at the preserve the next morning."

Nick, fully intrigued, urged the deputy to continue. "What else?"

Ratchett said the tip had gotten him thinking. "The van's description reminded me of the vehicle I'd pulled over on Bay Port Road that very afternoon. Guy was driving with a brake light out. Said he was heading to Mud Creek to check the fishing. But nothin' unusual about that," Booger said. "Guys come up here all the time to see what's bitin'—plus, if you're from the city, sometimes you just like to go for a nice ride in the country. Didn't think much of it at the time."

Now Nick was getting excited. "Please tell me you wrote the guy a ticket and got all his information."

"Well, not exactly," J.R. said, some of the steam coming out of his voice. "I let the guy go with a warning. Seemed like a nice enough dude, though almost too nice—real chipper and syrupy. So, anyway, after I got the tip, I decided to check my dash cam to get another look at the van."

"And what did you find?" Nick asked, almost breathless.

"Jackpot! Got his license plate number and a nice picture of the back of the van. Checked with the state, and the van is owned by Larry O'Brien of Bay City." Booger's voice was now filled with triumph. "Checked in with the Bay County Sheriff's Department as a courtesy, told 'em I was going to pay Mr. O'Brien a visit to chat about his little trip into our neck of the woods."

Nick thought it was a great idea and asked Booger to let him know when the lawman came to Bay City. "I'll tag along with you, if you don't mind."

One problem, Boog said. "Van was reported stolen this morning. What a coincidence, huh?"

Chapter 18
Friday afternoon
Bay City, South End

At three in the afternoon, Nick and Dave pulled up to the home of Andrea Pilinski on Lincoln Avenue in Bay City's South End. After their chat with the priest that morning, Dave had called Andrea and asked if she would be willing to talk with both reporters. They wanted to clarify parts of her earlier interview.

She'd agreed, declaring this to be an uncanny coincidence. "I was just picking up the phone to call you, when the receiver rang in my hand. I have some interesting new information I think you'd like to hear."

Andrea had also asked if Natasha would be joining the reporters. "She's delightful and cute as a button," she added, noting that the two of them made a nice couple.

Regrettably, Tasha was at work, Dave said, and could not join them. "But thanks for asking about Tasha—I think she's terrific too."

Earlier, Dave had called one of the Noon Optimists Club officers, someone he knew and trusted. Awhile ago he had written an extensive feature article about her and the positive work done by the Optimists. Now he hoped to get her opinion about Andrea's state of mind.

She'd answered on the second ring with "Well, hello, sunshine!" Dave, of course, couldn't see Rene Jones, but when he heard the greeting, he immediately thought of her arms stretched out for a hug.

Dave identified himself and she remembered him instantly. "Why, Dave, how in the heck are you? How lucky am I to get a call

103

from the great Dave Balz, reporter extraordinaire. Why, I could reach right through this phone line and pinch your plump cheeks."

Dave hoped she was referring to the cheeks on his face. Hearing her singsong voice brightened his day. He decided not to waste time with chitchat. "Hey, Rene, always great talking with you too. Got a question for you about one of your members," Dave said. "I hope we can talk today in complete confidence. I'm not calling you for a comment in a newspaper article. I'm looking for background info, and I felt pretty sure you would have it."

Rene readily agreed. She trusted Dave after the article he'd written about her, and she knew he had an excellent reputation; he liked to party but was one heck of a good reporter. She asked how she could help him.

Dave explained that he had interviewed Andrea Pilinski for a story he was working on, but another source suggested her information might be unreliable. "I thought she had a great interview and I believed she was a straight shooter, but then I was told that she sometimes hears voices and tends to exaggerate. The source said he thought her mind might be slipping. You know Andrea from Optimists. What do you think?"

Rene hesitated before responding. "Look, we all lose a little when we age. Happens to just about everyone. I absolutely love Andrea. She's such a positive force, especially for children's programs. But ever since Ralph died, I've noticed that she's more forgetful. That's also when she started saying, 'Don't you know' at the end of sentences. She started that because Ralph was almost noncommunicative in his last years. And yes, I think she still talks to Ralph, and in her mind, he answers."

"What do you think? Can what she says be trusted? Have you ever known her to make up stories or be untruthful?"

"No, she's not a liar," Rene said. "If she told you something, then she believes it to be true. She is such a sweetheart. She never swears or cusses. Telling a lie would be so unbecoming of her, she just couldn't do it."

Dave wondered about her hearing. "Ya know, sometimes when we get older, our vision slips, our memory slips, our hearing slips. Hey, it's happening to me. What about Andrea? Have you noticed anything about her hearing?"

Rene shook her head no, then realized Dave couldn't see it. "Haven't noticed anything, but then I haven't had her vision or hearing tested either. This is so darned tricky to answer."

Dave could hear papers being shuffled in the background. He feared Rene was about to be pulled away from their conversation. He thanked her and encouraged a return call if she thought of anything that might be helpful.

Now Dave was relaying the gist of their interview to Nick, whose face twisted up in a knot when he heard it. "That sounds like a less-than-ringing endorsement of Andrea."

"Let's talk to her, see what you think," Dave said. "Plus, she says she's got new information for us."

The reporters rang her doorbell. Andrea greeted them with a smile and seated them in front of the fireplace again. Her silver-blond curls bobbed as she walked to the kitchen. She wore a colorful Easter sweater today and dark slacks with bunny slippers.

When she returned with a tray of fresh coffee and Easter cookies, the reporters dug in as if they were, well, starving stray dogs in Bay Port.

While they chowed down, Andrea spoke. "Who wants to go first? I'm so excited to tell you what I learned, don't you know."

Dave brushed crumbs off a burger grease stain on his new shirt. "Why don't you start? We can listen while we chew, mostly silently."

Andrea beamed like a first-grader at show-and-tell. "I know the name of your murderer."

Nick nearly choked on his cookies, and Dave almost tossed his. "What?" Nick managed to blurt out. "Say again, please."

Andrea was so pleased with their reaction that she giggled and hopped in her seat.

"I said I know who your murderer is," she said, clapping her hands as if she were applauding her accomplishment. Nick thought she was acting like a giddy child. "Want me to tell you?"

The reporters looked at each other. Had Andrea solved the mysterious murders? Nick encouraged her to continue, and Andrea wiggled in her seat and took a deep breath.

With a smile as big as a banana, Andrea blurted out, "Your killer is Natalie O'Brien."

The last name rang a bell with Nick. He'd just heard from Booger that the owner of the suspicious van in the Thumb was named O'Brien. "You seem certain, Mrs. Pilinski," Nick said.

Dave put down the cookie he was gnawing on and nodded in agreement. "How can you be so sure?"

Andrea's smile did not fade. She said she'd identified Natalie O'Brien as the killer because she'd recognized the woman's voice after hearing her speak out loud during a meeting of the Noon Optimists Club.

"Her voice was clear as a bell, and just as distinctive as when I heard her in the confessional at St. Clementine's. I knew it was her right off, but then she used that word and I positively was certain."

"What word?" Dave asked.

Andrea hesitated and shifted in her seat. "Begins with *H* and ends in double hockey sticks. Natalie said it in church, don't you know, and she said it the same way at Optimists. I know what I heard." Andrea leaned back and nodded at the reporters, confident she had solved the crimes for them.

Nick let her assertion settle. Andrea was confident in her hearing, but he wanted to know more about the reports of her hearing voices. Hearing was one thing; voices another. He knew pressing her might cause her to go silent but decided it was worth the risk.

Nick said he and Dave had heard reports from people who knew Andrea that she sometimes heard voices. Could this be one of those times? he asked.

"Why, that's silly. Who in the world told you that?" Andrea looked down at her hands, which were folded in her lap. "Sure, I still hear Ralph's voice from time to time. He hasn't been gone that long. We were married for eons. He didn't have to talk to me to communicate. I understood him even when he didn't speak, don't you know."

Andrea didn't like thinking about the possibility she might be unstable. Few of her friends knew that Andrea's mother had been committed to the Eloise Psychiatric Hospital in Westland, Michigan, during the 1940s, one of the largest mental institutions in the country. Her mother had spent much of her miserable adult life restrained in a padded room. Finally a lobotomy had left her in a hazy stupor.

What Andrea feared most was the idea that her mother's madness would one day plague her or her children or grandchildren. Until now, few had questioned her mental fitness. Discussing it made her uneasy.

Dave said he and Nick were told that Andrea sometimes had difficulty remembering things and tended to exaggerate. Why would people say that?

Now Andrea's eyes flashed, and she stiffened in her seat. She took a long sip of coffee, then leaned toward the reporters, pointing an angry index finger at them.

"See, this is exactly why I did not go to the police," she said. "Every time an older person is a bit forgetful or has trouble hearing, people jump to the conclusion that they are losing their minds. Not everyone over seventy has dementia. Not every aging person has Alzheimer's.

"This is pure and classic ageism." Andrea's voice rose to emphasize her point. She had given this idea considerable thought, and unloaded. "If I had gone to the police, they would have done exactly what you are doing. Question my sanity, and then start wondering if I'm a threat to myself. And then the first thing you know, they send a social worker to check up on me, and that gets the neighbors yacking. It happened to Ralph. I'm not losing it, and I am not out of my mind. This really upsets me."

Nick said the reporters did not mean to hurt her feelings. "Please don't feel offended," he added, hoping to calm her. "We're here talking with you because we believe you have something to say, but we have to check it out." He explained it was their job as reporters to ask questions, then question the veracity of the information they received.

The reporter's words acted like a salve on an open wound. Her breathing slowed, and she folded her hands in her lap.

Nick asked how she'd learned of Natalie's name if she only recognized her voice, and Andrea explained how she'd gone back and checked Registration. "I jotted it down so I wouldn't forget."

This revelation alarmed Nick. He grimaced. "If you know Natalie's name and what she looks like, is there a chance she knows who you are?" he asked. "Did she follow you into that meeting to learn your name? Is a murderer tracking you now?"

Fear rolled over Andrea's body. She hadn't thought of the encounter at Noon Optimists that way. Now a killer probably knew her name and might have discovered her home address.

Dave asked if Andrea had told anyone what she overheard in confession besides them.

"Yes, I told the priest, don't you know?"

It turned out she'd also told the priest the name she had given them. "He's my priest. I confide in him. I called him this afternoon—I wanted him to know I wasn't making up what I overheard in confession. Finding out her name was my proof to my priest that I'm not losing my mind."

"I think you need to be careful," Nick said, scooting his chair closer to her. He wanted to make sure she understood his concern that she might be in danger. "If Natalie O'Brien is a murderer, she may know your name and now your face. Do you have a relative or a friend that you could stay with awhile?"

The questioned riled her, causing a resurgence of the jabbing index finger. "I won't be chased out of my home by that—that horrible person. Not only is she a confessed killer, but she also uses bad words in church and the confessional. What kind of lady does those things?"

Dave asked Andrea if she owned a weapon. Had Ralph kept a handgun in the house? Could she defend herself if needed?"

"A gun? Oh my goodness, no. What in the world would I do with a gun? Lordy, Lordy, Lordy."

Chapter 19
Friday evening
St. Clementine's Catholic Church

Natalie O'Brien waited in the shadows, just beyond the beam of the streetlight. So far, nine good Catholics had entered the front door of St. Clementine's to participate in Friday night confession. She watched patiently for about ninety minutes, counting as each of the nine left the church.

A cold, light rain fell as day surrendered to the night. No cars were approaching the hundred-year-old house of prayer. Natalie flipped a lit cigarette into the street, grabbed her handbag, and headed for the front entrance, hoping Father Bob hadn't left.

The dimly lit church was quiet, no others in sight, though the priest's confessional light was still on. Natalie shot for the nearest booth and entered, clicking the door shut behind her.

Father Bob slid the wooden window open with a thud. "Yes, my child. What's troubling you today?"

Natalie cleared her throat and leaned in toward the mesh screen. She could hear his shallow breathing and smell his aftershave, which was different from Wednesday's.

"Hello, Father, I'm back to finish our discussions from earlier in the week. Did you miss me?"

"Why yes, I did, Natalie. I hoped you would come back," he said in a soft, even tone. "Shall we pick up where you left off?"

The priest's words caused her head to snap upright. "How did you know my name?"

"Ah, I believe it came up the other night," the priest said quickly. "I could be wrong, but I think you referred to yourself in the third person and your name popped out."

Natalie was not convinced. She'd been extra careful not to reveal too many details, including her name, to the priest.

"Ah-h-h, I don't think so," she said. "I didn't give you my name. It must have come from Andrea Pilinski, that nosy bitch. She identified me at Optimists, didn't she? Now, she thinks she'll blab to the whole world. This is the end of the road for Andrea."

Father Bob replied matter-of-factly, trying to cool her animus toward the South End grandmother. The sweet little old lady was not a threat to anyone, he said. She was extremely lonely since losing her husband to dementia, and most St. Clementine's parishioners thought she'd begun to decline. "Slipping, as they say," the priest continued. "She talks to herself, hears voices, has discussions with her deceased husband. Not a threat." He encouraged Natalie to talk about herself: "What about you? Have prayer and meditation prompted a change in your heart? Are you truly sorry for these mortal sins, and are you ready to atone for what you did?"

Natalie asked if they could step out from the confines of the confessional to talk face to face, but she did not wait for a response. She plunged through the door of the telephone booth–sized box after several minutes. The priest followed suit.

Natalie took control of the discussion. "After our last meeting, I had the distinct feeling you were turning my way. You revealed that you'd been violated repeatedly and that you understood me. I thought we had made a connection."

"My child, my child—"

"Don't give me that 'my child' shit. If you understand me and what happened to me, why can't you give me absolution?"

"To receive forgiveness, you must be truly sorry and atone for your sins," he said, sitting in a pew sideways and facing her. "That's the only way for you to recover from this tragic period in your life. I'm curious." He motioned for her to sit down, and she did. "Why didn't you go to the authorities and allow them to punish the men who hurt you?"

Natalie stared at the priest. Then she burst out laughing. "Father, you've got to be kidding. Real estate is how I make a living. It's how I feed my kids. Tell me, what homeowner would be willing to list their place for sale with me after I allowed a felonious assault to take place on their property? What do I say to a homeowner? 'I lost control of the situation and let a brutal gang rape occur in your daughter's bedroom.' How do you think that's going to fly?

"And my broker!" She laughed out loud. "He's from the Stone Age—a knuckle dragging Cro-Magnon. He thinks I'm flirtatious. Even if I was wrapped up head to toe like a tamale, he'd say I asked for it."

Natalie was revved up now. "What about my daughters, my family, my friends? If I report this, my life is over, and my rape kit ends up in an evidence room with hundreds of others. Then I have to live with the shame and stigma. No way could I go to the cops."

Father Bob asked how she'd tracked down her assailants.

"I told my sister and brother about it—Kate went crazy, said we had to track down and kill the SOBs. She called Larry and told him. Larry held me and cried. He said he'd kill them for me himself. Then he kissed my head." Natalie said that Kate had gone to the convenience store at the corner near the house where it had happened. A hundred bucks cash in the attendant's hand got her access to the tapes from the day of the assault. Kate wrote down the plate numbers of the vehicles that had followed Natalie, then turned the numbers over to a police dispatcher, one of their brother's connections.

"Larry tracked them down," she said. "Don't ever underestimate my brother. He caught them as they cornered and attacked another

Realtor in Saginaw County. Larry said he broke up the assault. Both guys were naked, the poor girl out cold. He knocked 'em out with a tire iron, tied 'em up, and then took 'em in the van to the farm in Kilmanagh."

Father Bob asked what became of the woman.

"Larry called me, and I took her to the hospital," Natalie said. "She couldn't stop crying. She thanked us. I left her. She never reported the assault."

What about the men? Father Bob asked if she'd watched them die. "Did that give you pleasure?" His voice was still calm, measured. He crossed his legs and draped one arm over the back of the pew.

"Yes, it did." Natalie started to stand up but then retook her seat to continue the description. The priest wanted details. She was happy to oblige. "During the assault, one of the guys choked me until I passed out. After I came to, the other one put a pillow over my face and said, 'This is what it feels like to die, bitch,' and then he pressed the pillow down until I was sure it was over. I thought about my girls, I prayed for it to end—even if they killed me. That's how bad it was."

Natalie said watching their deaths was exhilarating, a feeling she'd never experienced. "I made sure they saw my face and heard my voice when I told them, 'This is what it feels like to die,' and then my brother squeezed the life out of them. It was glorious."

Father Bob stood and paced the aisle.

Natalie could see he had become upset by her revelations. She remained seated and took a deep breath. "And we are not done," she said. "The third body that turned up in the Thumb the other day, well, he was a serial rapist, but he's out of business now. He was killed by Dr. Y. Larry took out my attackers and enjoyed it, but he didn't want to kill anyone else."

As for Dr. Y, she said, it had started where most evil things begin: a search on the internet. At first they'd searched for assassins on the dark net, but the O'Briens couldn't afford them and couldn't verify that the assassins weren't cops. But Larry had stuck with it, bouncing from chat room to chat room until he found a group of sexual assault victims who called themselves the Vigilant Vigilantes, a network of women across the country who were fighting back against rapists.

"We use burner phones to make contact, then encrypted emails with coded language. Nothing traces back to us. Dr. Y, who may be male or female—we don't know—killed our last rapist, and now Dr. Y's scheduled to kill two more pieces of human scum. Then Larry will whack off their pee-pees and chop them up with a commercial ban saw at the farm. We need to improve body disposal methods, but we will get better each time. We are committed to making a difference, no matter what it takes."

The casual discussion of killing made Father Bob shaky. He sat down again, holding his chin in his right hand, staring at the floor. Natalie thought he might throw up right there in the middle of St. Clementine's.

The priest held up his hands. "You must stop killing, please. This can't go on. Turn it all over to the authorities. I will help you."

Natalie, arms crossed, shook her head. She said she and her siblings were done waiting for the police, the courts, the legislature. "They're all pretty much run by men, and guys obviously don't give a shit—at least enough to make it stop," she said. "You want statistics? The numbers are horrifying. In India, gang rape, family rape, revenge rape are almost as prevalent as sunshine. We're not as bad as India, but we're close.

"And it goes on and on. We're not putting up with it. We're tracking down rapists, verifying their illegal acts, and having them killed so they can never hurt another woman again."

Chapter 20
Friday night
Bay City Blade newsroom

Nick checked his watch. He'd just finished writing his story for Saturday's newspaper and was about to send Tanya a text to meet him at O'Hare's Pub for some fun after a long, hard week, when his cell phone rang. He did not recognize the number but decided to answer anyway. He was glad he did.

It turned out to be Greg Szemanski, who had delivered the first box to the *Blade*.

"Hi Nick," Greg said. "You said to give you a shout if I ran across the guy who asked me to deliver the box. Well, he's here right now, sitting at the bar watching the Tigers on the big screen."

"Where's here?" Nick stood up and clicked off his computer. He was ready to run.

"Oh yeah, sorry. I'm washing dishes at Jake's Corner Bar. I spotted the box guy when he came in. Checked him out from the kitchen through the servers' window. It's him. No doubt about it. Sitting at the end of the bar, right under the TV."

Nick thanked the young guy and snagged his jacket off the back of his chair. "I'm on my way over now. Keep an eye on him till I get there. You got his name?"

"No clue what his name is," Greg said. "Hey, and one more thing. Your doctor friend. Great guy. Like a magician. Changed my diet, gave me miracle cream. I can almost see what I look like in the mirror now. Before, it was just big red bumps and pus. Can't thank you enough. I got an outside shot at getting a girlfriend now."

"Welcome," Nick said as he hit the exit from the newsroom. Jake's was about six blocks from the *Blade* front door. The reporter decided to hoof it because he figured he'd have trouble finding a parking spot near the popular hangout.

While he walked, he revised his text to Tanya: "Hi sweetie, meet me at Jake's Corner Bar. I'm on my way there to meet a guy who might be one of our murderers."

Inside Jake's, a standing bar with a footrail lined the outside walls. Tall tables and chairs dotted its interior. Big-screen TVs displayed sports games from across the globe. At the back of the cavernous room, a long sit-down bar gave way to the kitchen entrance. Nick spotted Greg peeking through the servers' window. The kid nodded toward a big man with curly dark hair who was watching the Detroit ballclub.

Nick studied the man for a few moments, then took the empty seat next to him. He ordered a pint of Guinness, hoping the selection would prompt a comment.

It did.

"Now, there you go," the stranger said. "That's a real pint you got your hand around. Here's to ya."

The two clinked glasses. The big guy toasted: "A wise man invented beer. A smart man drinks it. But a genius drinks Guinness."

They laughed and pounded down the dark, heavy beer and wiped their chins with their sleeves. Nick asked about the ballgame.

"Like always, Tigers need a rally. Their pitchin' has been crap all night."

"Same old story," Nick said.

The two men sipped Guinness until Nick decided to swing for the fences and see if he could connect for a homerun. It was a hunch, but he really hoped the guy sitting next to him was Larry O'Brien.

"I gotta ask. Are you by any chance Larry O'Brien?"

The big guy with curly hair laughed out loud and faced Nick.

"You a bill collector?"

Nick shook his head no. Said he and a couple of his friends were trying to locate Larry O'Brien from Bay City, who'd owned an old van until this morning, when it was stolen. Wanted to chat with him.

"Nope, not me," the guy said, foam clinging to his upper lip. He concentrated on the big screen. "I'm Irish, but I'm not an O'Brien. Sullivan is the name. Call me Big Jim, my friends do." He stuck out his paw to shake.

Nick smiled and identified himself.

"Hey, you that reporter from the *Blade* who solves all the murders?" the man asked, giving the game a momentary break from his attention. "You're pretty famous in this town. Nobody wants Nick Steele on their tail. That what you want O'Brien for?"

Nick said he simply wanted to talk with Larry O'Brien. But he was also hoping to meet the man who'd had a small box delivered to the *Blade* earlier in the week. "Did you have that box delivered?" Nick asked, sitting sideways in his chair. "I have a source who says you gave the box to a high school kid."

"Oh, a source told you, huh?" A smile spread across the big man's face. "Would that source be a pimple farmer who wears a Central High hoodie?"

Nick didn't respond to the question, but Sullivan kept going. He acknowledged that he'd given the box to the delivery kid but did not know the man who'd first handed it to him.

"I was sitting right here on this very stool and some guy—he sat in your seat—had the box on the bar," Sullivan said. "Guy said he had to catch a flight from the Midland airport, but he needed to get the box to the *Blade* before he left town. And it had to go to you specifically. Said it was worth a hundred bucks to him.

"So, I said I'd get it to the *Blade*. He handed me a C-note and almost ran out the side door of this place. I had another beer and asked the kid, who was working in the kitchen at the time, if he wanted to make fifty bucks."

Nick listened intently. "Wow, that's wild. Either you or the delivery kid could have tossed the box and pocketed the cash."

The big guy stuck his chin out and poked his thumb into his chest, proclaiming, "I'm a man of my word. Told him I'd take care of it, so I did. The story I saw in the paper said it ended up as evidence for those murders. Is it true? The rumors? I must ask, was it two sets of balls?"

"No, but you're close," Nick said, laughing. "Can't reveal the box contents right now, but it will be published in the paper at some point. Let me ask you this, could you identify the man who gave you the box? Can you describe the guy?"

"Sure could. He was sitting next to me as close as you are. He was short and fat—a walking jelly donut. Dark hair, beard, dressed like he worked over at the Chevy plant in Bay City."

Nick thanked him and offered to buy him a pint. Sullivan held up his right hand and begged off. Said he was already late getting home; perhaps they'd share a brew another time.

"Got to go, mate," he said, standing and offering his hand for a second shake. "Have a great evening and guide those Tigers to a W."

Nick nodded, and watched the big man cut through the kitchen to the rear exit. Immediately Greg slunk out of the kitchen and asked Nick if the man was the guy he was looking for.

"No, turns out he was the wrong Irishman. But it was good talking to him. He says he took the box from another man before he gave it to you for delivery."

Greg frowned. "I don't remember him with anyone else before he gave the box to me," he said. "What did he say his name was?"

"James Sullivan."

"Odd." Greg pointed toward the kitchen with his chin. "I heard the cook say, 'Good night, Larry' when he walked out the back door."

"No shit," Nick said, just as Tanya slid onto the barstool beside him.

"Is that any way to greet your wife?" she asked. "I thought you were meeting one of your killers."

The reporter laughed. "I think I just did. Larry O'Brien is one cool dude." He gave Tanya a quick recap of the meeting, noting how the man had slipped away as Big Jim Sullivan.

Tanya ordered a vodka martini and grabbed Nick's arm as it rested on the bar rail, pulling him closer to her.

"This story is getting to you, isn't it? I can tell," she said. "You are restless at night, like you're tussling with a gorilla. I haven't seen you this upset since the Suzie Alvarez story."

Nick gave Tanya a quick peck on the cheek. She was perceptive and tuned into what made his clock tick. "Yup, you're right," he said in a low voice. "It's getting under my skin for a lot of reasons. I abhor the idea of rapists targeting and attacking women, with few or no repercussions. I loathe the notion that vigilantes are taking the law into their own hands because they know the law is not protecting them. And it absolutely is driving me crazy that body pieces are being dumped in the area where I grew up."

Nick asked Tanya for her thoughts. Did she believe the rapists were getting what they deserved? Were the Vigilant Vigilantes like the Lone Ranger from the Old West, doing a messy job for which folks should be thankful?

"Rapists should face the full force of the law," she said, pausing to say goodbye to Greg, who had been called back to the kitchen. "But they should not be summarily executed by people who decide on their own that they can pick up a weapon. Nick, you know that too. Vigilantism is not the answer. We need tougher laws and punishment, not killers taking the law into their own hands."

The couple sipped their drinks and snuggled closer.

Nick said he'd started looking into the problem the Vigilantes said they were trying to solve. The numbers were shocking: a recent report suggested more than five thousand rapes every year in Michigan, and that didn't include the number that went unreported.

"It's like that all over the country," he said. "I had no idea. I need to talk to the C-Man. That's got to be part of our investigation. Our story won't be complete without it."

The two ordered a second round. Tanya urged him to let it go for the night.

"Otherwise I'm in for another night of tossing around," she cooed into his ear. "Remember, we're hosting breakfast in the morning. We can talk more about it then. Let's have some fun tonight, just you and me."

Amen, Nick said, and gave her another quick smooch.

Chapter 21
Saturday morning
Nick and Tanya's apartment

Nick fried up a pound of bacon and scrambled a dozen eggs for breakfast. Tanya burned toast and poured juice. Dave would join them as soon as he picked up Natasha and a fresh bowl of fruit from City Market, and Mrs. Babcock had promised to bring her famous sticky buns and a big pot of fresh-roasted Columbian coffee.

Nick had called the breakfast meeting, hoping it would provide a productive setting to discuss the Thumb murders. This had become a complex case, and a brainstorm was in order.

Dave arrived first. He surprised Nick and Tanya by donning a clean T-shirt for the occasion. Baggy gym shorts, wrinkled and stained with what all hoped and prayed was peanut butter, and flip-flop sandals completed the look. As usual, he bubbled with energy. Tasha brought in the fresh fruit. She wore jeans, a Grateful Dead concert shirt, and tan sneakers. Makeup was, as usual, a stranger to her face.

"Hey guys, check this fruit out. These strawberries are almost as big as my fist," Dave said, exaggerating only slightly. He grabbed a piece of toast off the plate Tanya had prepared. "And where's that killer coffee from Mrs. Babcock? I need a little help beating back this hangover."

"Gee, is this the first time you've had to tangle with a bad hangover?" said Tasha, taking a juicy bite of strawberry. A tiny trickle of red dripped to her chin.

Without prompting, Dave licked it off and kissed her on the cheek. "And it's a safe bet the hangover this morning won't be my last," he said.

As if on cue, Mrs. Babcock appeared in the doorway, lugging a coffee urn and a bag of sticky buns. "Did I just hear my name? I'm by myself today—the smell of bacon frying is driving Jenni crazy. I didn't want her drooling and slobbering while we ate. That's Dave's job."

Jenni was the landlord's black lab, a sweet pooch that loved bacon almost as much as life. Mrs. Babcock, dressed in her daisy-covered housecoat and slippers, set the urn on the dining room table and started drawing cups of the hot, dark brew. Her salt-and-pepper hair had been freshly and elaborately coiffed. Her only makeup was a touch of light pink on her lips. Cat-eye glasses rode the sharp ridge of her nose.

The landlord thanked her hosts for the meeting invitation. "I've been reading all about it in the paper, so I'm excited to learn the background of what's going on. Please, let's update. Where are you with this case?"

Nick always enjoyed Mrs. Babcock's take on the stories he developed. She had a no-nonsense view and a good feel for the thoughts of Bay Cityans. Nick opened the discussion by saying he'd met and talked with one of the case's prime suspects—Larry O'Brien—without realizing it. The group laughed and teased Nick about the legendary investigative reporter getting outmaneuvered at a bar.

"Never fear," he said, working the eggs over with a spatula. "I'll catch up with Larry O'Brien, and the next time he won't jump the hook and take off."

Dave, finishing his last bite of toast, told them he'd set up a meeting between Andrea Pilinski and Bay City's Officer Dan Quinn. The South End woman had been reluctant to go to the police regarding what she'd overheard in the confessional, but the reporters had encouraged her to do it now that Natalie O'Brien, the confessor, had probably identified her.

"Quinn is going to her place this afternoon to get a statement," Dave said. "I briefed him on the situation and told him she was super-sensitive about being accused of getting old and losing her mind. Quinn said he would tiptoe around her. Imagine that, if you can: a six-foot-seven, three-hundred-pound lug on his tiptoes, prancing around her living room."

The image was a hoot. Dave said he'd also picked up new information: DNA testing had confirmed that Terry LeForte's penis tip was in the first box sent to the *Blade*, and his remains were found with Guy Devereaux's in that farm field near Pigeon.

Dave had learned from Quinn that the memory card found in LeForte's shaving kit turned out to be a horror show. "Tasha, Tanya, Mrs. Babcock, if you don't want to hear the next part, I can save it and tell Nick later."

The women stared at Dave, then glanced at each other. Tanya spoke. "We're big girls, we can handle it. And I have a hunch what's on the memory card, but please, do tell."

Dave nodded. "The card was filled with images of women being brutally assaulted by two men, presumably LeForte and Devereaux. Not a Hollywood production, so Quinn says the images are dim and grainy."

"How many images, how many different women?" Nick asked, stirring the eggs to keep them from burning. "Are any of the women recognizable?"

Dave said Quinn did not know the number. "Dan says he counted nine different women being assaulted, but could not continue watching because the photos made him sick to his stomach. He does think one of the women is Natalie O'Brien, based on the photo we lifted from her website."

Nick shook his head in disgust. "So, one of the animals took photos of the assaults and the other took trophies—undergarments—from their victims. You know, I hate to say this, but I'm glad they're gone. Lowest of the low. No place for them among the civilized."

Mrs. Babcock suggested that Nick was not alone in that thinking. "A lot of people around town believe taxpayers were saved a bunch of money for not having to pay for prosecution of those two. The executioners did us a favor."

Tanya interjected, saying vigilantism could not be encouraged. "We talked about this last night, Nick. A civil society requires us to follow the law, not take the law into our own hands."

The kitchen quieted as the new information settled over the group, the sizzle of frying bacon the only sound. Nick suggested they focus their energy on Natalie and Larry O'Brien, who were their best suspects, though no direct evidence tied them to the case.

"I checked out the website you asked me to review, Nick," Mrs. Babcock said. The retired real estate broker kept her license active with a few sales each year, and her finger on the pulse of the market. "Natalie O'Brien looks professional—she's a riser. Her sales go up each year, now selling $2.5 million annually, and she's getting repeat customers and regular referrals. I'd say she's on her way to making real estate a top-notch career."

Tanya asked if her website indicated that Natalie specialized in selling a particular kind of property. "I guess I'm wondering how the two creeps found her, singled her out of the mob of Realtors in Bay County?"

Most of Natalie's sales were residential, Mrs. Babcock said. "Single-family homes—she puts together specialized financing for a wide range of incomes. Looks like she's trying to help families buy and sell. Very solid."

Nick brought two platters to the table: one overflowing with crispy bacon, and the other brimming with steamy eggs from Farm Crest Foods in Pigeon, where 850,000 hens cranked out product every day.

"I thought having eggs from Pigeon was appropriate this morning since we are talking about the horrific crimes in the Thumb," said Nick, who thought it prudent to put the trays down and get out of Dave's way when he decided to feed.

Dave had a horrible habit of shoving food in his face before sitting down at the table. Today was no exception. The reporter loaded a tall stack of bacon strips and eggs onto a single piece of toast. He pinched the bread edges together and shoveled the pile into the open space between his cheeks. Food bits flew.

Tasha tugged Dave's forearm and whispered, "Slow down, you're killing appetites all over the place."

Unfazed by Dave's frenzy, Tanya asked Mrs. Babcock if violence against Realtors was a new phenomenon.

"It's gotten worse in recent years," she said, lacing her scrambled eggs with ketchup. "You never know who is going to walk in your office door or who is calling on the phone. Don't have to tell you how many wackos are out there. Some of the people you meet are downright frightening."

Tanya asked what she did, as a broker, to help female agents guard against attacks.

"Rule number one—never meet someone you don't know alone in an empty house or building," she said. "We always tried to piggyback when meeting clients the first time, and checked in with each other hourly when out in the field doing showing or listing appointments alone.

"Rule number two—no physical contact outside of a firm handshake. I had one agent who was a young mother and felt like she had to hug everybody who walked in the door. Bad idea. It finally registered for the agent when one of the wackos stalked her, hanging out in the office parking lot and following her around," she said. "We had to call the police, who told him to knock it off. Stay professional, keep a distance."

Tasha, relatively new to the group, cautioned against victim-blaming. "Nobody asks to be assaulted, nobody invites rape. The agents are trying to do their jobs and make a living."

Mrs. Babcock nodded in agreement, saying she'd always encouraged her agents to be aware of their surroundings. "You have to think of it as a soldier walking into a combat zone. They aren't asking to be shot at, but they sure better be ready for it." The landlord examined a piece of bacon as if it were caviar, then devoured it, chewing as she thought. "I'll never forget my own close call. I was young and stupid. I was supposed to show a family an unoccupied home, but only the husband showed up—he said a conflict arose and the Mrs. stayed home with the kids. Well, I didn't sweat it, just went ahead with the showing. But as we went through the property, I could feel his eyes on me, up and down, staring at me like I was naked. Creepy. I also had the feeling that he was trying to corner me as we walked through the house, so I kept moving with a good distance between us.

"All of a sudden, I had this foreboding feeling—something bad was about to happen, and I started looking for the nearest exit. That's when the doorbell rang. It was an agent who had arrived early for the next showing. Boy, was I glad to see her. I welcomed her in and got rid of the creep. Never heard from him again, but I was way more careful after that."

Nick looked up from his plate, which was less than half full, and asked if the violence against Realtors only involved women.

"I've never heard of a female client sexually assaulting a male agent, but we do occasionally hear of clients getting so angry, they lash out with a slap or a punch," she said, pushing the eggs around on her plate with her fork. "When people think they've been wronged or cheated, anything can happen. This is America, Nick, and we're a violent people." The landlord finished breakfast by chomping on a last piece of toast. "Unfortunately, when folks take matters into their own hands, the results can be ugly."

Chapter 22
Saturday afternoon
Lincoln Avenue, Bay City, South End

Youngsters with long sticks pretended to fish from a pothole in the street near Andrea Pilinski's driveway. They were dirty and dripping with sloppy mud. They also were having a blast. Watching them warmed Natalie O'Brien's heart almost as much as the spring sunshine. She had been casing Andrea Pilinski's home since early morning, sitting in her vehicle under shady trees just down the street from the woman with the silver-blond curls.

Since Father Bob had confirmed for Natalie that Andrea had identified her, Natalie had been unable to sleep or find rest. Inside, she was outraged that the little old grandmother had listened in on her confession and was now interfering with their mission.

Granted, Natalie realized she had been loud in the confessional, but Andrea could have walked away once she knew it was no longer a private discussion. Instead Earmuff Lady had listened to the whole thing, making her a busybody in Natalie's mind—a busybody and a danger. Andrea was a threat to the O'Briens, and now she needed to be neutralized.

So far, Natalie had only seen Andrea once. The grandmother had stepped out of her garage with a rake and cleaned leaves from her flowerbeds under her front window for about twenty minutes. Then a Bay City Police Department cruiser had pulled up in front of her house.

Natalie watched a giant emerge from the vehicle. Shaggy blond hair and a walrus mustache made Officer Dan Quinn look like Hulk Hogan without the rippling muscles and fake tan. Andrea stopped raking and greeted the patrolman. Natalie rolled down her front windows, hoping to hear what the two discussed.

After quick introductions and chipper small talk, Quinn told Andrea that he was present to take a statement. Andrea responded with a smile. "Dave Balz from the Blade said you'd be dropping by this afternoon."

"Damn it, damn it," Natalie said to herself after seeing the smile brighten Andrea's face. She slammed her palms on the steering wheel. "She blabbed to the paper and now she's spilling her guts to the cops."

As Quinn followed Andrea into the house, Natalie rifled through her purse to find the burner phone. Time to call Larry, she thought. He needed to know that cops and at least one reporter were getting close to their tight circle.

Larry picked up just before the call went to voicemail. "Yeah, what's up?"

"I'm sitting outside the home of the woman who overheard my confession," she said, keeping her eyes trained on the front door. "The cops just arrived, and I heard her say a reporter told her they would be coming by for a statement. Ho-ly shit!"

Larry didn't respond. She figured he was thinking—Big Bro always got quiet when his brain kicked into overdrive. She didn't press him. Not wise.

Finally he spoke. "I was ambushed by a reporter at Jake's last night. Sat down beside me, tried to get me drunk, hoped I would spill. Came right out and asked if I was Larry O'Brien, but I stiff-armed him and bolted when I could. They're getting close, no doubt about it."

"Oh my God! It's gotta be all speculation. They're guessing. We've been careful."

"Not careful enough." Larry sounded deeply troubled. "I think it's time for me to disappear. Heading out in the morning. Going to visit an old army buddy up in the wilds of Alaska till things cool off here. We should all take a step back and hunker down. This will blow over."

Natalie's brain raced as she listened to her brother. He'd always had a good sense of timing. Knew when it got too hot and knew when it was time to hit the road. But what about her and Kate? Natalie had already decided they would not run.

"I get it," she said, pulling a cigarette from her purse and lighting it with one hand. It was a bad habit she had rekindled after her assault. She blew smoke up toward her open sunroof. "Me and Kate are going to sit tight and wait this out. If they had anything solid, the cops would be putting cuffs on us. No, hell no, I'm not worried."

That was a lie, and the O'Briens knew it. Larry said he would be in touch. He urged Natalie to be cautious. "No matter what, walk away from that grandma. Let it go. I'm getting a bad vibe off you when it comes to her. Start your vehicle right now."

"Okay, thanks," Natalie said. "Good luck. Be careful." She clicked off the burner phone and stuck it back in her bag, then checked her watch. The kids had scattered when the police cruiser pulled up. Now the street was quiet, and the giant cop was still inside the house. Fifteen minutes had passed. What could they possibly be talking about for all that time?

Natalie decided to drive around the block to see what Andrea's place looked like from behind. Slowly she pulled her van out into traffic, not wanting to draw attention to herself. At Nineteenth Street she made a right-hand turn, then turned again onto Sheridan. She parked when the back of Andrea's home came into view. A neighbor stood atop a short ladder, trimming a maple tree. No one else was in sight.

The home directly behind Andrea's featured a hedge that ran along the driveway to the rear property line they both shared. Perfect cover to get into Earmuff Lady's backyard, Natalie thought. She checked her watch again and fired up another cancer stick. Twenty-five minutes had passed now since Andrea invited the policeman into her home. She decided to go back to her previous spot on Lincoln Avenue to watch the front door.

As she parked, the big policeman ambled down Andrea's front steps. They spoke briefly before he walked away and coiled his body back into the cruiser. Andrea did not smile or wave goodbye. Natalie thought she looked like she was about to cry.

When Andrea went back inside and closed the door, Natalie reached for another cigarette, though the last one still burned in the ashtray. One puff and she started to relax. Her legs had stiffened from so much sitting. She used the burner to call Kate, but there was no answer.

Soon Andrea's garage door opened, and the big yellow Caddy inched down the driveway. Natalie came alive. She waited for several minutes, watching the hulking banana move toward Nineteenth Street. When Andrea was out of view, Natalie drove back to Sheridan Street and parked. No movement in either direction—a quiet Saturday afternoon.

She slipped out of her van and scooted along the hedge. The street remained clear. When Andrea's backyard came into full view, a smile erupted across the Realtor's face. "Aha, that's how I get in!"

Natalie retreated to her van. Soon Andrea would no longer be a problem.

The big yellow Caddy's brakes groaned as Andrea ground to a halt in front of the Bay City Blade, which was closed Saturdays except for the newsroom, production department, and pressroom. Like always, those operations remained on 24-7 cycles. The news never stopped. Only losers quit chasing it.

But when Andrea discovered the front door to the newspaper was locked, she let out a soft wail and pulled out her cell phone to call Dave Balz. The reporter answered right away. Dave and Nick were working in the newsroom on the second floor of the paper.

"What's up, Andrea? Did you meet with Officer Quinn?" he asked, eager to learn how the interview had gone. "Is that why you're calling?"

Andrea let go of giant sobs that had been building since the policeman left her home. "Boo-hoo, boo-hoo! It was horrible!" She tried hopelessly to hold on to her tears and snot. "I know he thinks I'm crazy. Boo-hoo, boo-hoo!"

The reporter looked out from the window of the second-floor conference room and spotted the top of her vehicle. "I'll be right down to let you in. Nick and I are working on our stories for Sunday's paper. We can talk now."

Andrea felt better immediately. She gave Dave a big hug when she entered the Blade building, and wiped her nose on his shoulder, which he didn't seem to mind at all. Just another mystery stain on another dirty T-shirt.

Nick joined them in the first-floor conference room. The reporters asked her to tell them what happened.

"The officer seemed like such a nice young man," she began, dabbing at her eyes and nose with a linen handkerchief. "But his first question threw me for a loop. He asked, 'When did you first realize you were losing your mind?' It got worse from there."

Nick slapped the top of the table with an open hand. "So much for tiptoeing. Quinn can be a real clod sometimes."

Andrea bawled, her chest heaving. "See, I told you this would happen. I should never have bothered talking to the police. He asked when my hearing started to go bad. When did I start hearing voices? How long had I been talking to my dead husband? He wanted to know if it was Ralph's voice I heard during the confession." Her tears flowed. "I got so mad, I started to ramble at him. He called it ranting. When he closed his notebook and stood up, I knew it was over. I know I sounded like a raving lunatic. I'm sorry. I couldn't get him to believe me."

"It's okay, Andrea," Dave said, touching her shoulder gently. "It was miscommunication. We'll talk to Quinn and smooth it over. Next time I'll stick with you when you meet with him. He can be intimidating. A big lug."

"Oh, no. There won't be a next time," she said. "I can't take the humiliation of being laughed at just because I'm getting older. I am not losing my mind or hearing. I know what I heard. I should have kept my mouth shut and tended to my own business."

Andrea stood up from her chair and walked stiffly toward the door, her face red and puffy, her eyes all cried out.

As she left the building, the reporters went back to the newsroom to finish their work. Nick said he would check with Quinn later.

"I hope she's okay," Dave said. "I hate to see her so upset. Hope she gets over it."

Andrea would never get over it.

Chapter 23
Sunday morning
Lincoln Avenue, Bay City, South End

Mass on Sunday mornings was scheduled for eight and ten o'clock at St. Clementine's, with coffee and cookies served afterward. Natalie O'Brien figured Mrs. Pilinski to be a traditionalist, so she expected the woman to attend the later celebration. Natalie was correct.

At half past nine, the big yellow boat on wheels crawled down Lincoln Avenue, then turned right on Nineteenth Street before making a hard right on Sheridan. Natalie had parked in the service alley that split the homes on Lincoln and Sheridan. When Andrea passed Natalie's vehicle, the Realtor hopped out of her van and crept down the alley toward the hedge that led directly to Andrea's backyard. Today she wore a dark jacket and sweatpants with sneakers. A foot-long wire garrote remained coiled in her jacket pocket. She did not carry a handbag.

Natalie headed straight for the home's old-fashioned coal chute, which had been converted to allow firewood to be dropped into the basement. The door to the chute was held tight by a hook-and-eye latch—no lock. That's what had caught her attention.

Within minutes, the Realtor released the hook and slid into Natalie's basement. She pulled a small flashlight from her jacket and used it to guide her way up the stairs to the kitchen. Her plan was to catch Andrea by surprise in the garage when she returned from church. With the garrote, the end would be fast and quiet. Natalie would return to the house after dark to dispose of Andrea's body.

She checked her watch. She had at least one hour before Earmuff Lady returned from Sunday mass, and the Realtor was curious

Murder, so Sweet

about Andrea's place. She wandered through the house, careful not to touch anything, checking out photos, mementos, how the home was staged. Natalie discovered Andrea's bedroom near the back of the house. A large four-poster bed rested in the center of the room. Photos of Andrea and Ralph and their offspring covered the walls. Too bad Andrea had been so nosy and blabbed, Natalie thought. Now she had to go.

Natalie returned to the garage and found a narrow hiding place behind sheets of plywood just inside the garage door. She needed a smoke, but it would have to wait. She wriggled in behind the lumber, trying to get comfortable. All she had to do now was wait for Andrea to come home.

Great plan, but it fell apart when Andrea returned home from church with a friend, another little old grandma riding shotgun. From her hiding spot, Natalie watched the two women, dressed in their Sunday finest, including pillbox hats with veils, get out of the Caddy and dodder up the stairs into the house.

"Damn, damn, damn," Natalie said to herself. She would have to shift to Plan B, except there was no Plan B. She escaped out a rear door, pulled the coal chute door closed, and slipped back down the alley.

Andrea Pilinski made a fresh pot of coffee. Her friend of thirty years, April Flowers, sat at the small white kitchen table. The two had been talking on the telephone for days. April was the one person Andrea could trust. She'd told April about the confession she had overheard and her subsequent discussions with Father Bob and the reporters. After the debacle with Officer Quinn, April had urged her friend to go on the offensive.

"I know you are telling the truth," April said. She lifted her veil and removed the pillbox hat, gently pressing her hair back into place. Andrea joined her at the table. They nibbled on biscuits and washed them down with hot, fresh brew. "And now you tell me you've seen the woman who confessed to murder watching you on this street. She's stalking you. If the police don't believe you, you're in big trouble. You're going to be her next victim."

Andrea relaxed despite April's words. It was such a relief for her to hear a friendly, supportive voice. She'd known she could count on April. They had helped each other when they lost their husbands, they rejoiced together when their grandchildren were born, they were good practicing Catholics, and they both were Noon Optimists.

"April, you are so right," Andrea said, stirring a squirt of cream into her coffee. "Anyone who brags about killing two men and says she would do it again without hesitation is dangerous. But when you say I should go on the offensive, what do you mean?"

"It would be a mistake to allow your stalker to make the next move." April said she'd given Andrea's situation a lot of thought. Everyone in America had the right to protect themselves and their property, she said, noting those rights were protected by the Constitution. "I think I've got the perfect solution for you," April told her. "You need protection. When we finish our coffee, I'll show you what I have in mind. My grandson will be here shortly to help. Trust me, this will work. I have it at my home, and so do many others."

Andrea reached across the table and covered April's hand. "Thank you so much. I knew you'd come through for me."

At eleven thirty Sunday morning, Nick and Dave stood across the street from St. Clementine's, watching Father Bob greet his flock after mass. The reporters wanted to make one more run at him to see if he could provide any information they could use. Nick could easily see that Father Bob was admired. The priest moved among his parishioners with ease, smiling and chatting with each family as they munched cookies and slurped coffee.

After about fifteen minutes, the priest spotted the reporters. Nick waved, but Father Bob did not respond or acknowledge them. When it appeared as though the clergyman was moving toward the church entrance, the reporters scooted across the street to catch him between parishioners and the safety of the church building.

"Father Bob, would you have a minute to talk?" Nick called out, quickening his steps. "It's important."

Dave added that a member of St. Clementine's might be in danger. His remark caught the attention of several cookie eaters who were watching the two strangers chase their spiritual leader. The words also stopped the priest in his tracks. He waited for the guys to catch up to him.

"Not you two again," he said, crossing his arms, a Bible in his right hand. "I told you when we spoke last that I would have nothing to say to you. That hasn't changed. I can't speak with you about any of this."

Nick nodded, saying he understood—but changing circumstances had forced the reporters to return to him. "We have new information that we believe you should be aware of—in fact, you may already be aware of it."

The priest looked exasperated. "You guys just don't quit, do you? We've been down this road before, and it's a dead end. My vows prevent me from talking about anything that happens in the confessional. No matter what I hear, I cannot act on it."

Dave, slightly breathless from hustling across the street, leaned in toward the priest, hoping that others would not hear. "Father, we have reason to believe that Andrea Pilinski may be in grave danger. She is a sweet little old lady. She doesn't deserve this."

Nick continued, pushing harder. "We believe that Andrea overheard Natalie O'Brien's confession of murder and may now be in danger because Natalie has identified her. We believe you are aware of this."

Father Bob held up his hand in protest. "Please, no more. We are done here."

A burly parishioner stepped close to the three men. He asked the priest if there was a problem. "Are these two guys bothering you? You want me to run them off?"

A quick shake of his head signaled the priest was okay. "Thanks, Jerry, but it's all good. These men will be leaving momentarily."

Nick took a final shot. "Father, if you are aware that Andrea is in danger, you must speak up. Go to her and caution her or alert the police. If you don't and something bad happens, her blood will be on your hands. Can you live with that?"

Without saying a word, the priest turned and walked away.

Jerry held his ground, facing the reporters. "I think that's it, guys. Father Bob is a holy man. Don't try to take this any further, or I will be forced to stop you."

The reporters watched the priest enter the church and close the door. By now the parishioners had mostly scattered. Nick and Dave retreated too.

At three that afternoon, Father Bob turned his powder-blue Volkswagen Beetle onto Lincoln Avenue. As he pulled up to the

Pilinski residence, April and her grandson backed down Andrea's driveway in his pickup truck. The women waved and wished each other a blessed day.

The priest approached the passenger's side of the truck to speak with April, who rolled down her window. "Wonderful seeing you at Mass this morning, April," he said. "Next time, bring your grandson. Always looking to see young people in the church too. We need his youthful exuberance."

April smiled and her grandson was polite, nodding at the priest and thanking him for the invitation. He called Father Bob "Padre."

"Awful nice of you to stop by Andrea's," April said. Her pillbox hat and veil rested in her lap. "Is this a special occasion, Father?"

"Happened to be in the neighborhood, just thought I'd drop by and say hello." The priest smiled broadly and waved. "You two didn't stay for cookies and coffee this morning. Wanted to make sure everything was okay."

"Oh yes. Everything is good," she said. "My grandson offered to help Andrea with a little home improvement project. Didn't take long at all. Nice seeing you, Father."

As the truck pulled away, the priest spun around to see Andrea rocking gently in her porch swing, a grin almost as big as her Caddy spread across her face. She motioned for the priest to join her. "Warm sunshine over here, Father. How delightful of you to stop by."

They exchanged small talk, mostly chatting about the St. Clementine's Women's Auxiliary. He thanked her again for organizing and leading the weekly cleaning of the church.

As Father Bob stood up to leave, he mentioned that two reporters from the Blade had visited him that morning after mass.

"For some reason, they are very concerned about you," he said, stretching the boundaries of honesty. "They told me you might be in danger, so I thought I should pass that along. Are you still living alone here? Ever think about having a friend or relative stay with you for company?"

"No, Father. Not necessary." Andrea used the tips of her toes to push the swing. "Ralph and the Lord are watching over me, don't you know," she said.

Suddenly he envisioned her late hubby and Jesus forming a tag team like professional wrestlers to watch over and protect her.

Andrea asked the priest if he'd like afternoon tea or a soft drink. She offered to fetch a tray of fresh Polish pastries that she'd picked up from the Krzysiak House Family Restaurant, a Bay City South End institution.

"Thank you, but I'm still stuffed from the cookies after Mass this morning," he said, stepping off the porch. "Nice chatting with you, Andrea. I'll be on my way."

Andrea walked with the priest to his VW Bug. "I realize you can't talk about anything that goes on in the confessional, but I don't want you to worry about me. That horrible woman I overheard, that Natalie, isn't going to harm me. Don't give it a second thought, Father. I've got a surprise for her."

Chapter 24
Sunday night
Lincoln Avenue, Bay City, South End

Plan B turned out to be a variation on Plan A. Natalie decided she could not wait another day to dispose of the threat. After dark, the Realtor left her daughters with Kate without revealing her plans. When the woman returned to Lincoln Avenue, she found a place to park under a burned-out streetlight three doors down from the Pilinski home. It was cold and quiet now that night had finished swallowing the day.

She would wait until well after Andrea's lights were turned out, then make her move to the basement coal chute. Having already used the chute as a point of access would make it easy for her to get back into the house without attracting attention.

One by one, lights flicked off inside homes on both sides of Lincoln Avenue. Once Andrea's house lights went out, Natalie waited at least half an hour to allow the woman to fall asleep for the last time. The garrote was still in her pocket if needed, but Natalie now planned to smother the old woman with a pillow. She was half Andrea's age and was confident she could overwhelm her. Plus, if Andrea's body was discovered without visible injuries in her bed, it might be assumed that the elderly woman merely passed in her sleep.

Natalie checked her watch. It was time to move. She scanned the homes on both sides of the street—quiet, dark. No one in sight in any direction. The Realtor had already disabled the van's interior dome light. She slid out of her seat and closed the van door without letting it slam.

In the distance, a dog barked. Natalie heard its owner order it to shut up or risk another beating. She moved slowly and quietly, her soft-soled sneakers padding the sidewalk as she reached Andrea's driveway. Natalie stopped and scoped the area. So far, so good.

The Realtor slid along the driveway until she reached the end of the garage and backyard. She waited at the corner of the garage, again scanning her surroundings. Half the homes in the neighborhood had nightlights glowing over their backyards. Andrea did not have one, but her neighbor did. It provided just enough light to find the coal chute door.

Natalie unhooked the chute door. She held the flashlight in her mouth and slid through the chute, dropping to the basement's cement floor.

Her heart pounded. Being in the basement now was different than earlier in the day. This time her nemesis was upstairs, hopefully fast asleep and drawing her last breaths.

Natalie turned the light's beam on the basement stairs and swept it across the floor, making sure nothing blocked her path. When her breathing evened, she stepped toward the stairway. She was halfway up when the flashlight slipped from her hand and tumbled to the cement floor with a double clank.

"Damn it, damn it!" she said to herself. Andrea's bedroom was directly above. Natalie strained to hear any movement from the main floor. Nothing. Dead silence. Her heart felt like it was jumping out of her chest. How could she be so stupid and clumsy? she thought.

Luckily the flashlight had not gone out when it hit the floor, and Natalie recovered it. When she reached the top of the steps, she waited until she was certain everything was quiet, nothing moving in the home.

As she nudged open the basement door to the kitchen, Natalie could see that a nightlight had been left on in the bathroom, which was at the end of the main hall. The kitchen was clean and tidy, as it had been earlier. She moved through the dining area and stopped in the living room, searching for a cushion. Bingo!

A big, cushy pillow filled a corner of the sofa. She picked it up with a gloved hand and punched its center with the other. This would work nicely, she thought. She checked for the garrote, her backup weapon. It was still coiled in her right-hand-side pocket. Again her heart jumped like it was on speed.

Natalie checked the street from its front window. Dead still. She focused on Andrea's bedroom door at the end of the hall. The hardwood floors squeaked beneath her feet. Each step echoed the familiar groan of shifting weight on ancient oak flooring. Why hadn't she noticed the squawking wood during her tour of the home before? Natalie slowed and stepped gingerly down the hall, pausing between each creak to listen, praying it didn't cause the crazy old bag to come whirling out of her bedroom with a baseball bat.

When she could see Andrea's door, another sound broke the night silence. Snoring, light and steady, oozed through the entryway—three long bursts, then a snort. Andrea was a mouth-breather. She was sleeping hard, Natalie thought, and the squealing floors did not seem to stir her. Natalie's shoulders loosened. She took long, deep breaths to steady her nerves. This was going to be as easy as one, two, three, she thought. Step in, find target, cover whole head with pillow, and apply all her weight until the old girl went limp.

The metal doorknob was cold to her touch. She prayed it was unlocked. It was. Natalie twisted the knob, and the bedroom door opened, metal hinges creaking. She pushed into the room. One step inside, and then a loud blast—BOOM!—echoed through the house on Lincoln.

Chapter 25
Early Monday morning
Lincoln Avenue, Bay City, South End

When Nick and Dave reached Andrea Pilinski's home just after one in the morning, it was surrounded by cars and trucks with flashing lights. Police and EMS hurried between their vehicles and the crime scene. Dogs barked. Residents yacked at each other on the sidewalk and rubbernecked for a better look inside the windows of the house.

An investigator told the reporters they could not go into the home while it was being combed for evidence. Nick asked what had happened. Word over the police scanner indicated a shooting had occurred but offered little detail. A security guard at the *Blade* had heard the report and alerted news reporters.

"The homeowner is still there," the officer said, looking back at the house, where every light was lit. People could be seen milling about inside. "An intruder was shot, and I think she's dead, but don't quote me on that."

Nick glanced at Dave. "Wow, I did not see that coming," he said. "Never figured Andrea had the wherewithal to shoot someone down—even an intruder."

Dave agreed. "Where did she get a gun, and how did she learn to use it? Andrea told me she didn't have a weapon."

The officer held up his hand to slow the reporters down. He said it wasn't as simple as that. "There's a big problem for Mrs. Pilinski. She booby-trapped her bedroom. Booby traps are illegal. They got the prosecutor out of bed on this. I think she's going to be arrested and charged."

The reporters were stunned. How in the world could this

elderly grandmother—so sweet and gentle—set up a booby trap that worked? Dave asked the officer if Andrea had an accomplice. Were any others being arrested?

The officer said Andrea had told investigators a friend and her grandson had helped her set up the elaborate rigging. A holstered weapon was screwed to a bedpost. The handgun had gone off when the door opened.

"We have their names," the officer said. "Prosecutor's going to have to decide charges for them too."

Nick asked about the victim. "Just a wild guess here, but is the deceased Natalie O'Brien?"

"Can't confirm that because next of kin have to be notified," the officer said, looking over his shoulder to see if anyone was listening. "But that's a good guess. Right on the nose. Sounds like you are familiar with the players."

Nick nodded. He asked if there was a way the reporters could get into the house to see the booby trap. It would make a great photo and illustrative diagram, he thought.

"Nope, no way. Not until they are done investigating."

The garage door was open, and a light illuminated the big yellow Caddy. It also showed Nick that the door inside the garage leading into the kitchen was open. While the cop strung yellow crime scene tape around the yard, Nick darted through the garage and peeked into the kitchen. No officers in sight. The reporter inched his way inside the home and through the doorway leading to the hallway and the living room. There, at the end of the hall, was a body sprawled on the floor, covered with a sheet. It was directly across from the bedroom.

In the living room, two officers quietly informed Mrs. Pilinski of her arrest. They recited her Miranda rights and advised her what was about to happen. Then they escorted a weeping Andrea out of her home.

While all attention was on her, Nick slipped down the hallway, stepped over the body, and looked into the bedroom. Two cops hovered over the booby trap, photographing every part of it. Fingerprint dust hung in the air. They hardly noticed Nick in the doorway, perhaps figuring he was one of the investigators.

The reporter used his cell to take photos of the elaborate weapon and its sophisticated rigging—cable running from the handgun's trigger through four pullies to the door. No way Andrea set this up herself, Nick thought. As he retreated, he snapped off pics of the covered body in the hallway and a long bloodstain on the wall. It appeared as though Natalie was struck by a high-caliber round and driven out of the bedroom, then hit the opposite wall before slumping to the floor. The sight nauseated the reporter.

Outside the house, applause and whistles filled the air. Neighbors covered the front lawn, cheering for Andrea as she was brought down her front steps.

"We're behind you all the way, Andrea," said an elderly man dressed in PJs and a robe. "You had every right to defend yourself. Yahoo! Good for you."

Others clapped and shouted encouragement. An older woman said her son was an attorney and he would meet her at the Bay County Jail. "We'll get you out, Andrea. You did nothing wrong."

It was pitch black, but spotlights from the police vehicles illuminated the Polish grandmother and the path in front of her. She was handcuffed behind her back and looked terribly distraught. Dave approached as she was led to the open door of a police cruiser.

"Mrs. Pilinski, are you okay? Were you hurt during the attack?" Dave asked, walking sideways to keep up with the officers. "Did Natalie O'Brien break into your home?"

The elderly woman, dressed in sweatpants and a pullover, stared at Dave in disbelief. "I was simply protecting myself and my property," she said, sniffling. "That horrible woman broke into my home and came into my bedroom to hurt me. It's in the Constitution. April said we all have the right to self-protection. I did nothing wrong."

One of the officers wedged himself between Mrs. Pilinski and the reporter. Dave tried to talk over the bulky cop. "Did April help you set up the booby trap? Did she give you the weapon?"

The officer responded for her. "That's enough questions for now. You can talk to her later." He guided the top of Andrea's head as she slid into the back seat. Dave felt sorry for the woman. He could see her, caged and cuffed in the rear seat, weeping and unable to blow her own nose.

Nick and Dave split up to interview neighbors on the street. They hoped to learn more about what had happened earlier in the day leading up to the shooting. Interviewing them while events were still fresh and they were wide awake—and before they could talk to their own attorneys—would be their best opportunity for detailed information.

One neighbor reported seeing a strange van parked in the service alley. When Dave checked out the tip, police were already getting ready to load it onto a tow truck. The officer in charge of the van search told Dave they'd found the victim's ID and a couple of schoolbooks. The ID had confirmed what the shooter told police about the intruder, the officer said.

Use of the words *victim*, *shooter*, and *intruder* regarding O'Brien and Pilinski caught Dave by surprise. He was still processing their roles in this tragic event.

Nick interviewed a neighbor who had known the Pilinski family for twenty-five years. Good salt-of-the-earth types, the man said. Friendly, helpful, quiet neighbors. He leaned against a street sign to steady himself as he talked with the reporter. "I saw that van this morning and didn't think much about it," he said, motioning toward the service alley with his chin. "People pick the alley all the time, especially before trash day."

The neighbor said he saw nothing unusual at the house either. "Andrea had some people over after church this morning, but that's typical for a Sunday."

Nick asked if he knew the visitor.

"April Flowers, who I believe she knew from St. Clementine's," the man said. "Later April's grandson stopped by. Boy, he's a lowlife. April has had him at the homes of several people on this street and Sheridan. He brought a box into Andrea's place today. I thought maybe he was doing home repairs." Later in the afternoon, he added, a priest had stopped by Andrea's. "Hard to miss that white collar stepping out of a powder-blue Bug."

While Nick finished his interview, Dave called Officer Dan Quinn, who had not been among the police at the crime scene. The reporter thought Quinn should know what had happened, but he also wanted to find out more about the policeman's interview with Andrea on Saturday afternoon.

Quinn was groggy but came alive when Dave updated him on the events on Lincoln Avenue.

"Booby trap? Ouch!" the policeman said. "Illegal in all cases. I'd say she's probably looking at some kind of murder charge, and conspiracy if others were involved. I knew she was stressed out to the max when I talked to her."

Dave asked for more detail about the interview with Andrea. Was it as bad as she'd told them?

"The woman was definitely rattled and scrambled," Quinn said, stifling a yawn. "But I wouldn't say she's losing her mind. Hell, I know some reporters who are way crazier than her." The big cop waited for a reaction from Dave, but none came, so he continued. "Sure, she's aging, but aren't we all? I thought she was drifty but okay."

Dave asked him about Andrea's assertion that she'd overheard a confession of murder at St. Clementine's. If Andrea felt threatened by Natalie O'Brien, wouldn't that be an argument for self-defense in relation to the booby trap?

"Oh, I believe she thinks she heard something," Quinn said, "but the question is what. I've been going to confession most of my life. Sure, you sometimes hear bits and pieces. So what? Everybody lies in the confessional. I'll bet priests don't believe half the crap they hear, but that's their job."

Dave thought Quinn's version of Andrea's police interview was substantially different than the grandmother's. Perhaps she'd misunderstood him, or maybe he'd misread her. Either way, it was the little old Polish lady who had been carted off to jail.

Quinn thanked Dave for the call but said he was going back to sleep. "You can read my report on Andrea if you like. I'm sure the prosecutor will be looking at it soon."

Chapter 26
Monday morning
Bay City

While Andrea Pilinski faced charges of second-degree murder and conspiracy to commit murder in the booby trap death of Natalie O'Brien, a much harsher and more immediate brand of justice was being handed out to men in two nearby Michigan cities.

In Midland, police discovered the body of Randy Cobb in a trash bin at the end of a downtown alley. The bin had not been emptied in a week, so it was unclear how long Cobb's lifeless body had been in the garbage, though it had started to reek.

When his body was pulled out, police found a tourniquet around his upper right arm and a needle sticking out of it. After review, a medical examiner determined Cobb, a drifter and loner, had died from a hotshot of heroin and fentanyl.

In Genesee County, the body of Sean Davis washed up on the north bank of the Flint River not far from downtown. Wildlife had picked at the body, but authorities later determined an overdose of heroin and fentanyl had claimed his life too. Davis had been a General Motors employee with a lengthy record for assault and drug-related arrests.

The two deaths in separate counties raised few suspicions. They appeared to be junkies who had one fierce high too many and paid the ultimate price for it, not uncommon in today's drug-fueled culture.

But what authorities did not detect were the brands left on the bodies of the two dead men, who had been declared rapists by the O'Brien family and targeted for execution. If investigators had looked closer, they would have discovered a small set of initials carved into the armpits with a razor: "V V," signifying the tidy work of Dr. Y. The mysterious dark-net avenger had completed their task without raising concerns or alarms.

Dr. Y, responsible for Michigan and Ohio, was one of twenty-six V.V. executioners around the country. Dr. A covered Florida and Georgia. They were called doctors because they used a needle to inject their targets with a lethal chemical concoction of their choice. Their network was mostly women who worked hard to hand out justice to rapists, pedophiles, and kidnappers who had managed to escape the reach of the law.

The Vigilantes did their best to stay in the shadows. Most of their associates were like the O'Briens, regular people committed to wiping out the lowest of the low. The V.V. did not like the public display of scattered body parts and clipped penises that the O'Briens reveled in, but they tolerated it as long as the family did not threaten the overall organization.

Still, the group of assassins was not concerned about discovery, hiding behind a labyrinth of military-grade encryption, fake websites and email addresses, and coded messages. Natalie O'Brien had gone off the rails and paid the ultimate price for it, but the Vigilantes would remain firm and focused. They would look for others in this region of the country to replace the O'Briens.

Meanwhile, Natalie's killer was about to face Bay County justice.

In Bay City, a court-appointed attorney entered a plea of not guilty for Andrea Pilinski, who was so overwhelmed at the prospect of being paraded into the courtroom shackled and dressed in an orange jumpsuit that she could not speak for herself.

Afterward, the attorney told a small group of reporters assembled outside the courtroom that it was a clear case of self-defense and that no jury in its right mind would convict this grandmother.

The reporters knew Andrea's friends were hiring a first-rate defense attorney from Detroit. She would need one.

It took Bay City police most of the morning to locate Natalie O'Brien's next of kin. When they found her sister, Kate, the single mom of two was already in shock. She had just received word that her brother had been killed in a thirty-eight-vehicle pileup during a snowstorm Saturday night on a Canadian highway.

Kate had been trying to reach Natalie, when police and a social worker showed up. The double dose of bad news about Larry and now Natalie crushed their sister. She fell to her knees and pounded her balled-up fists on the floor. "Why, why, why!" she wailed.

Kate bellowed and sobbed, her whole body convulsing at the horrific news. She climbed to her feet, demanding more detail about Natalie. How had it happened? Where was she killed?

Police told her Natalie's death occurred inside Andrea Pilinski's home after an apparent home invasion, which caused Kate to shriek and fall to the floor a second time. "No, no, no! Not Natalie. I cannot believe this. It can't be."

But there was no mistaking it. Natalie was dead, shot in the chest, her children instantly orphaned. Kate told police she couldn't breathe and thought she was going to black out.

The social worker, who'd accompanied police to help break the news, comforted Kate and asked about the children. The distraught woman blurted out that her kids and Natalie's had already left for school. The social worker offered to stay to help Kate tell the children that their mom and aunt was dead. Kate, still numb from the shocking news, nodded her thanks. She wondered how in the world she would put the words together to tell them about what had happened to Natalie and Larry.

By the time the police were ready to leave, Kate had broken down completely. It had all gone too far, she said. She would cooperate with police after talking with her attorney. Now, she had to protect what was left of her family. She would make a deal with the prosecutors and do her best to rear her children and Natalie's.

Outside Kate's home, Nick sat in his gold Firebird and waited for police to finish their business. He hoped to talk with Kate before she had time to process, before she had time to talk with her attorney and clam up.

Once the police and the social worker had retreated from the home, Nick raced to the front porch. Kate, sobbing and heaving, answered by opening the door only a crack, the length of its chain lock. Nick identified himself. Without responding, she tried to close the door. Nick stuck his hand between the edge of the door and its frame, a risky move for a writer who valued his hands.

"Go away, I can't talk to you now," Kate said, her voice shaky.

Nick stood firm. "Please, hear me out. I think it's important that Natalie's side of the story gets told. We have interviewed the woman responsible for her death, and we've talked to the priest who originally heard Natalie's confession, but we do not have her own account of what she experienced leading up to today. People need to hear all of it. Will you spend a few minutes with me so people understand the full story?"

Kate's cycles of crying and sniffling slowed. "How do I know I can trust you? My family has fallen apart. I'm in a shitload of trouble here."

"I will make sure you are heard. It will be fair. I guarantee it."

Nick felt the pressure against the door lighten. Kate snorted and swallowed hard, then opened the door. Nick slipped into the entryway, pulled out his notebook, and reached into his jacket breast pocket to click on his recorder.

"I'll make coffee. You can sit at the table," she said, leading the way to the kitchen. "This is going to take a while."

Chapter 27
Late Monday night
Bay City Blade newsroom

The newsroom crackled with energy and tension as a dozen reporters compiled information, conducted telephone interviews, and pounded their keyboards to complete two packages of articles for upcoming editions of the *Blade*.

The first package, by Nick Steele and Dave Balz, would appear in Tuesday's newspaper. It would be an all-encompassing hard-news story of the events that culminated Sunday night, when Natalie O'Brien took a .45 caliber slug to the chest while inside Andrea Pilinski's South End Home.

Reporters were still working on the second package of stories, scheduled to run in Sunday's paper. It was a detailed look at sexual assaults in Bay County. The managing editor had assigned the stories to six reporters. The idea for the package had come from Nick Steele, who thought that sexual assaults and violence against women was a topic that needed to be reported. If rape had prompted vigilantism because a victim could not find justice, then Nick believed it worthy of investigation.

The package that Nick and Dave had written for Tuesday's editions would now get squeezed, punched, and turned upside down by copy editors before it went off to corporate attorneys, who were on-call and waiting to review.

FEAR and REVENGE
Blade probe reveals area murders fueled by raging emotions

By Nick Steele and Dave Balz
Blade reporters

This is the tragic story of two Bay City women caught up in conspiracies that ended in cold-blooded murder.

The first, Andrea Pilinski, worked with friends to kill or maim because of fear and intimidation. The second, Natalie O'Brien, participated in a plot with family members to kill for revenge after a sexual assault.

The result: Natalie O'Brien is dead and Andrea Pilinski is scheduled to stand trial in circuit court on charges of murder and conspiracy.

The worlds of the two women clashed violently Sunday night, when police say O'Brien entered Pilinski's home illegally to kill the one person who could link her to two killings in the Thumb. Police say Pilinski, fearful that O'Brien had stalked her and would kill her too, rigged her bedroom with a booby trap handgun with the help of friends.

Bay County Prosecutor Albert Skinner said the cases are the most wild and bizarre he's been involved with in the last twenty-five years. Skinner brought charges against Pilinski after careful consideration.

"There's no doubt about what happened," he said. "Mrs.

Pilinski has confessed to setting up a booby trap, and the people who helped her have pleaded to conspiracy charges for their role in the plot. Many will suggest that she had a right to defend herself, but the law is clear regarding booby traps. A jury and judge will decide her guilt and punishment."

Blade reporters interviewed dozens of law enforcement authorities, witnesses, and neighbors, friends, and relatives of O'Brien and Pilinski to compile this full story.

The story began two years ago inside a Bay County home listed for sale by O'Brien, a real estate agent and single mother of two. She had scheduled a showing of the home for a family interested in buying, but instead of a family, two men showed up at the unoccupied home.

The men cornered and overwhelmed Natalie, according to her sister, Kate, who agreed to be interviewed by the *Blade* for this article after reaching a plea deal on Monday with prosecutors in exchange for full cooperation in the case. She told authorities she did not physically participate in the murders. She will spend the next five years on probation, with two of those years on electronic monitoring.

Kate said the men, who had targeted and stalked her sister before trapping her alone, raped and brutally beat Natalie during a two-hour assault, repeatedly threatening to kill her.

When the attack was over, Kate said, Natalie did not go to police because she believed it would end her real estate career, the primary source of income for her family. Instead the woman had tried to live with and work through the physical and emotional trauma from the assault.

Over time, however, Natalie found she could not. Kate said Natalie finally broke down and revealed the assault to her and their brother, Larry, a retired firefighter and US Army Ranger.

"Larry and I were so angry about what the men did to Natalie that we decided as a family to track them down and deal with them," Kate said. "It wasn't that hard. Surveillance at a store gave us their license plates and identities. These men are lowlife scum. When we checked them out, we discovered they had stalked and assaulted other female real estate agents. We decided to kill them and make the world a better place."

Indeed, investigators say they have since discovered trophies that the men kept from the assaults. Police said one of the men, Guy Devereaux, kept undergarments from the rapes, and the other, Terry LeForte, captured images of the assaults. After photos and videos were analyzed, Natalie was believed to be among eleven women identified, police said.

When police recovered the box of trophy undergarments from the garage of Devereaux's sister in Saginaw, they discovered a drug deal in the works. They said the garage was being used as a "drive-up meth house." Drugs were created in the home's kitchen, and buyers would pull into the garage and purchase drugs in private from the homeowner, then pull away undetected, police said.

The undergarment evidence was confiscated and the homeowner arrested. Police said the drug house operation was permanently shut down.

Kate told police her siblings were surprised by how easy it was to take out two serial rapists. They decided, she said, to take their crusade to another level. Their new goal: dispose of more human trash. "Clean up Michigan" was their mantra. If authorities could not—or would not—stop the ongoing epidemic of rapes, then Kate said the O'Briens would.

"We knew we could do more, but we wanted help," Kate said. "Larry trolled the dark net until he found a sympathetic group, the Vigilant Vigilantes. One thing led to another, and we were put in touch with an individual who would do the actual killing if we researched and targeted the rapists. We have no idea who this person is—called only Dr. Y."

When asked for comment by the *Blade*, Prosecutor Skinner said he had never heard of the Vigilant Vigilantes. He said police recovered one of the burner cell phones and a laptop. The state police crime lab has the electronic devices under review.

"You can bet we'll take a hard look at the group," said Skinner, who is facing reelection next year. "The dark net is a dangerous place. We will go where we have to in an effort to fight crime."

Kate told the *Blade* her brother captured the two men and took them to a farm in Kilmanagh, a ghost town in the Thumb about forty minutes east of Bay City. Natalie insisted on taking part in the killings, Kate said, and their bodies were shredded by a commercial ban saw.

Larry dumped the remains of Devereaux and Forte in a manure slurry pit at a dairy farm outside Pigeon, Kate said. They were spread in an old sugar beet field by farmhands near Laker High School and later plowed under. Body tissue was unearthed during excavation last week, setting off a flurry of wild speculation and fears in the Thumb.

Once body parts were discovered, Natalie insisted on sending a message to the *Blade* with penis tips from the rapists. The message, addressed to Nick Steele, said "Stop the rapes." Kate said Natalie wanted that message—with the physical evidence—made public, a clear signal to sexual offenders that they were being targeted and a declaration of war to law enforcement and residents, warning that there would be a price to pay for ongoing violence against women.

"Natalie was so angry that the cycle of sexual assaults kept happening over and over again and little was being done to stop them," Kate said. "Natalie believed that if our government and law enforcement were run by women, then good ol' boy behavior would no longer be tolerated."

Police caught a break in the case when a piece of a thumb was recovered from the farm field. It yielded a print that led investigators to Devereaux. Before long, police identified LeForte as the second rapist in the case. *Blade* reporters, probing the histories of the two men, discovered the undergarments and photo trophies.

Huron County Sheriff's Deputy J.R. Ratchett said he and many others across the Thumb were delighted that the murders were solved.

"It was a real nightmare for us," the deputy said. "Body pieces turning up in the most unusual places. Wild animals feeding on human tissue. Can't tell you how much hysteria it caused us."

The remains of Ted Ferrier's body ended up in the Thumb's Sand Point Nature Preserve, Kate said. Ferrier was the test case for the O'Briens to evaluate how the arrangement with the Vigilantes would operate.

"Larry wanted to see their work before we gave them more serial rapists to kill," Kate said. "We targeted Ted, and Dr. Y took him out. Larry did the rest."

Pilinski entered the world of the O'Brien family when she inadvertently overheard Natalie's confession to a priest at St. Clementine's Catholic Church, according to Kate.

"We're Catholic, we're Irish. We are taught to feel guilty about our sins and confess them to a priest," Kate said. "Natalie got off on the revenge, but she needed to hear from a priest that she would be forgiven. He refused absolution because Natalie would not repent."

It got loud in the confessional, and Pilinski told the *Blade* she had clearly heard a confession to the murder of two men. But the woman was reluctant to speak up because she feared she would not be believed due to her age and the fact that her mother had been committed to a psychiatric hospital.

When Natalie realized that someone likely had overheard her confession, Kate said her sister became obsessed with Pilinski, believing the aging grandmother would put the O'Brien family in jeopardy.

"Larry and I both begged Natalie to forget about her," Kate said. "We tried to tell her that Pilinski was just a crazy old lady and nobody would believe her. But Natalie could not let it go."

The *Blade* reached out to Father Bob on two occasions, but the priest declined to comment, citing the seal of the confessional. He said all matters related to the confessional were confidential and could not be discussed.

Before long, Natalie began stalking the South End

woman. Pilinski said she'd observed Natalie driving in her neighborhood. That's when she became truly frightened, she later told police.

"My friend, April Flowers, said she had a solution," she told investigators. "I told her I could never fire a handgun or shoot someone. But April said I wouldn't have to if I let her grandson set up her home to stop an intruder. Self-defense is protected by the Constitution. April told me that. I should have checked. But you have to understand how afraid I was. I was desperate."

That's how Pilinski's home was booby-trapped. Police said there was no forced entry into Pilinski's home. Natalie apparently gained access by sliding down a firewood chute to the basement. She was shot once in the chest when she entered Pilinski's bedroom carrying a pillow. The intruder also carried a wire garrote, which was coiled in her pocket, police said.

Later, police learned that Flowers' grandson had rigged the homes of eleven other elderly widows in the South End with booby traps. Those killing devices have now been located and disabled as part of the Flowerses' plea deal.

Flowers and her grandson were charged with being accessories to murder and conspiring to commit murder. Prosecutors said they will receive reduced sentences for their full cooperation with authorities. The grandson will be on probation for five years.

When Larry O'Brien realized that *Blade* reporters had connected him and his van to the murders of the alleged rapists, Kate said he decided to flee.

"He was confronted by a reporter in a bar in Bay City.

> That freaked him out. He decided it was time to disappear until things cooled down. He told Natalie he was going to hang out with an army buddy in Alaska. That was last Friday. I learned Sunday night he was killed in a freeway pileup in Canada over the weekend."
>
> The O'Brien family is in tatters. Kate, the only surviving sibling, will end up rearing four children by herself.
>
> "We started out trying to avenge Natalie's assault," Kate said. "She was not the same person after she was attacked. It brought the monster in her out. She couldn't pull back. She became obsessed. It all got out of control. I'm so sorry for what happened."
>
> Andrea Pilinski told the *Blade* that her life, whatever was left of it, would never be the same. "Being sorry doesn't make it any better," she said. "Ralph told me just the other night that he hoped I learned a lesson. He said I should have minded my own business. I couldn't argue with him on that one."

The main "Fear and Revenge" article was accompanied by photos from the crime scene on Lincoln Avenue. Nick's pictures of the booby trap and an artist's rendition of how the device was rigged to fire when the bedroom door opened highlighted page one. A photo of Natalie's sheet-covered body was displayed on an inside page, with an accompanying article about why booby traps to kill or maim were illegal.

The *Blade* package also carried photos of each of the players in the story—Andrea, the O'Briens, the Flowerses, Father Bob—with short bios on each, detailing their roles in the case. *Blade* editors decided against publicizing more than the bare minimum of information about the men who planned and carried out the sexual assaults against women; they did not want to do anything that might glorify the men or their violent acts.

Running with the package was a "Coming Sunday" promotion, detailing what to expect that weekend: several articles about sexual assault, focusing on Bay County numbers and how those statistics figured into the state and national picture.

A sidebar would recount the stories of five local women and two men who had been assaulted in the last year. They had each consented to their names and photos being used with the sidebar, which detailed their gruesome and barbaric attacks. They said they agreed to go public in the hope that someone would come forward with information to help solve their cases. Though the seven had reported their assaults to authorities, no arrests had been made and their cases remained active investigations.

The Sunday *Blade* opinions page also would carry separate editorials condemning vigilante justice and rising sexual assaults against women. The opinion pieces decried the violence in both cases, urging an increase in law enforcement spending and a crackdown by the courts.

Nick and Dave were pleased with how their investigative package had turned out, but they knew the story was not over. They had to be ready to cover it.

Chapter 28
Tuesday afternoon
Dom Polski Hall, Bay City

As word of the *Blade* investigative package spread, the reaction was swift and loud. Outraged residents called the newspaper to declare their support for the eighty-two-year-old grandmother. They demanded Andrea's release from jail and all charges dropped—as if the *Blade* could make that happen with the snap of Dave Balz's stubby fingers. Still, the number of calls and their impassioned nature surprised many at the newspaper.

Public support for Andrea Pilinski was building. The local television and radio stations in mid-Michigan broadcast news reports about the *Blade* articles, calling details in the investigative report both shocking and horrific. They devoted an extraordinary amount of airtime to the sensational booby trap shooting that had claimed the life of Natalie O'Brien.

Media outlets in Detroit and Chicago, cities with large Polish populations, focused on the plight of Andrea, the sweet elderly granny whose only crime was protecting herself from a family of confessed serial killers. Some of the tabloid papers picked up on the story, declaring in blaring headlines that "Good Gal with Gun Stops Bad Girl with Garrote" while in defense of her home and life.

News reporters from across the country begged for jailhouse interviews with Andrea, but family members and attorneys advised against it until after the trial. The only news outlet excluded from this ban was the *Blade*.

Andrea insisted on the right to speak with Dave Balz, the one person who'd believed in her from the beginning. It was, after all, Andrea's initial call to the *Blade* tip line that had led to the unraveling of the story. Nick hoped she would continue talking with Dave.

The rise of the story on the national media radar suggested a real movement was underfoot. This was a story with legs, and the reporters would have to hustle to chase it.

So, when Nick and Dave received handwritten invitations to a South End meeting regarding the fate of Andrea Pilinski, they canceled their plans to celebrate at O'Hare's Pub on the west side of the city. The invitation offered the reporters high praise for their work and tipped them to a meeting at the Bay City Dom Polski Hall they "would not want to miss."

Before the meeting began, dozens of Pilinski supporters showed up at the county jail to chant their support for Andrea. They carried signs, sang songs, and marched back and forth in front of the building where female inmates were housed. They hoped their voices would bolster the South End woman, who until her arrest had never received even a parking or traffic ticket.

After an hour of spirited support, Andrea appeared at a jailhouse window, wearing bright orange and peeking through bars. She smiled and waved, not sure what else to do. Andrea's bail was set at $500,000, way out of reach for her family's modest means. She would be going nowhere for quite some time.

But that public display was just the beginning. More than five hundred people crowded into the open hall of the South End social club. The meeting was organized by Hazel Durant, one of Andrea's granddaughters. She did not want to see her "Na-na" pushed through the justice system and dumped in prison to die before her time.

Nick and Dave slipped into the back of the hall and did their best to blend, not wanting to draw attention to themselves as the rally built steam. Nick was amazed at the outpouring. "It's all happening so fast," he said. Nick figured the public displays of support would work in Andrea's favor because some of these folks could very well end up in her jury pool. He noted the speakers and the most visible supporters of Andrea—all fodder for interviews and fresh news stories later.

Hazel walked to the podium to address the raucous crowd, which buzzed with gossip about the case. A twelve-by-four-foot banner hung on the Dom Polski stage behind her. It read quite simply "Justice for Andrea!"

Hazel greeted the crowd to applause and cheers. "My grandmother should not be sitting in jail," she told them. "She should not be facing prison. We must rise up to save her. Justice for Andrea!"

The audience rose to its feet as one and began to chant, "Justice for Andrea! Justice for Andrea! Justice for Andrea!"

Hazel raised her hand to regain their attention. The flame had been lit. Now was the time to feed the fire. "We must be able to defend ourselves and our homes from those who would do us harm. And that—in its simplest form—is all my grandmother did. This is one of our basic rights, and it goes all the way back to 1776. We cannot allow Andrea to be railroaded. We must fight for her. Justice for Andrea! Justice for Andrea!"

The crowd, still on its feet, picked up the chant. As the fervor intensified, teenagers from All Saints Catholic High School carried a hundred cardboard signs into the gym. The hand-lettered placards declared their demand: "Free Andrea, Justice for Andrea, No Prison for Andrea." A campaign was in the works.

Hazel raised her hand again and introduced a series of speakers from organizations across the community that had a connection to Andrea and her neighbors: the Polish American Club, the Bay City Retirement Club, the Friends of AARP, the Sons of Warsaw Association, the Dom Polski Club of Bay City, and the Michigan Protectors of Polonia.

One after another, each speaker lauded Andrea and decried her circumstances. They pledged support for their sister and vowed to do whatever was necessary to gain justice for Andrea. Naturally, a fundraising basket circulated through the crowd. Dollar bills, hastily written checks, loose change, and promise notes overflowed the basket.

All Saints cheerleaders pirouetted and somersaulted into the gym. They had developed a routine for Andrea that included a series of flips, spins, handstands, and continuous twirling, which resulted in wild applause and cheering: "An-dre-a! An-dre-a! An-dre-a!"

Not to be outdone, the Catholic school's marching band high-stepped into the building, belting out a rousing rendition of "When the Saints Go Marching In" and, later, the national anthem of Poland.

During the rally, a vendor set up shop just outside the Dom Polski entrance. The aromas coming from his mobile cart put Dave's sniffer on high alert.

"I detect kielbasa and kraut," he said, his nose twitching high in the air like a beagle's. "Or maybe it's Polish sausage and kraut with onions and sweet mustard. It's got some zip to it."

Without waiting for a response from Nick, Dave elbowed his way through the crowd and chugged his block-sized body toward the entrance and the vendor. When he returned, crumbs littered his beard and mustard stained the new sports jacket he'd picked up cheap at Goodwill. "Definitely kielbasa, and the kraut was so fresh, I think it was still in the garden yesterday," Dave said, licking mustard from his fingers. "Did I miss anything?"

"More of the same. Amazing." Nick tossed Dave his handkerchief. "And yeah, you did. Something on your nose. I'm afraid to look more closely."

The rally for Andrea continued around them—the only thing missing from this setting were jugglers and magicians. Meanwhile, the organizers were hard at work putting together teams of protesters. While momentum built in Andrea's favor, they wanted to capitalize on the frenzy.

Hazel desired public support for Andrea throughout her incarceration and trial. Marchers would protest at the Bay County courthouse, the county jail, and City Hall (the seat of city government, not the east side downtown tavern called Old City Hall, where commissioners gathered and sometimes staggered out of after meetings). The plan was simple. Build public support for Andrea and pray it would be enough to swing a jury in her favor. In light of the overwhelming evidence against her, it was the family's only hope.

Chapter 29
One month later
Bay County Jail

As her trial date approached, Andrea Pilinski's celebrity grew across the community as well as inside the jail.

"Free Andrea" T-shirts and hoodies, with the eighty-two-year-old grandmother's angelic likeness on the front and back, were the hottest-selling garments in the Tri-Cities during summer months, when those communities rocked with festivals, concerts, and antique shows.

Everyone, it seemed, wanted to hitch their caboose to Andrea's steam engine. Poets waxed eloquently about the woman fighting for her freedom because she had the audacity to defend herself. A local R&B artist recorded a blues ballad about the lady he had dubbed the Polish Princess. The singer moaned and wailed about Andrea rotting in jail while her assailant "got what she deserved—a hot lead nighttime snack right in the old breadbasket."

Even inside the lockup, Andrea's star soared. Nick Steele received a tip from one of the jail guards he often used as a source that Andrea was now conducting classes for other female inmates and leading a nightly prayer session. The guard told Nick, "People are taking risks for her, and you hardly ever see that in a place like this. Usually nobody here gives a shit about anyone else."

Time for Dave to play his "Andrea invitation for interview" card, Nick thought. He pitched the idea to both the C-Man and the reporter at the same time, and later that day Dave had an appointment to interview Bay City's newest celebrity.

Previously Dave had visited Andrea in jail three times. Each meeting was a "Hi, how are you holding up in here?" discussion.

With each meeting, Dave could see that the accused killer was settling in and becoming more comfortable with her surroundings. By the second visit, her cheery smile and upbeat nature had returned.

So far, the grandmother had only two complaints at the jail. They were alleviated with a better mattress and new reading material. "The food is not home cooking," she told Dave, "but losing a little weight is a good thing."

Visitation at the jail was limited and controlled. Visitors and inmates were separated by Plexiglas, with communication through a screened voice slot. Privacy side panels separated visitors from one another.

When a guard brought Andrea into the visitation area, Dave thought the lousy-food diet at the jail she'd mentioned during an earlier visit was working. *Skinny* was the word that flashed to his mind. He stood from his chair when she entered the cubicle opposite him. She smiled. It warmed his heart.

"Hi, Mrs. Pilinski, you look great," the reporter said, leaning in toward the see-through shield between them. They both took their seats. "Are they treating okay Ok in here?"

The grandmother folded her hands on the table in front of her and winked at the stout reporter. "So good to see you, Dave. Obvious that you're not missing any meals! I'm doing just fine. The guards are very nice, and I've made some new friends here."

The reporter cut right to the questions that had brought him to the jail. He asked her about the tip Nick received that she was now teaching inmates.

Andrea shifted in her seat and peeked over each shoulder before speaking. Not exactly classes, she said, just offering some advice. She explained that a young girl had asked her a question and Andrea had tried to help. "She'd overheard me talking to another young woman about making clothes for my children and grandchildren," Andrea said, smiling again. "I had mentioned how much pleasure it gave me. Sewing and knitting were never chores for me, don't you know."

The inmates had asked the accused killer if she could teach them how to sew and knit. Andrea told the women she would be happy to, but needles and other sharp objects were considered jail contraband. Too easy to turn them into weapons.

"Well, the next day one of the girls brought me two used hypodermic needles, don't you know," she said, quietly. "I told her I thought I could knit with two pairs of needle-nose pliers, but those hypo needles are too sharp and dangerous." Andrea wiggled in her seat as she revealed what she had done to help her new friends. Three days later, she brought me a beautiful set of knitting needles and yarn." Andrea checked over her shoulders again, and whispered, "She said, 'Don't ask where these needles have been or how they got here, okay?'"

Since then, four other young women had joined their group, they'd acquired more needles and yarn, and now they were happily making blankies, mittens, hats, and snuggly toys for their children.

Andrea sat up straight in her chair and smiled broadly. Dave could tell she was proud of the accomplishment. "Knitting also has a calming effect, especially when you are doing it for someone you care about, don't you know. And these girls, they're single moms and separated from their children, they are so thankful for the little things."

Dave put his open hand up to the Plexiglas. They high-fived just as a guard wandered into view. He pointed to his wristwatch, indicating time running out.

"One more question for you," Dave said. "We also received a tip that you are leading prayer sessions. Is that true?"

"Oh, my goodness. It's nothing formal," she said. "I pray before bed each night. A couple of my knitters joined me. They're Catholic but had fallen away from the Church. I asked Father Bob if he could find me some rosaries, don't you know. Now five girls pray with me each night, and Father Bob is giving instruction to some of the non-Catholics. Not that big of a deal, really."

"No, Andrea, it is a big deal. You are truly inspirational," he said, rising to high-five her again. He told her that he and Nick would attend her trial, which was scheduled to start in a few days. "Good luck, Andrea. I'll be rooting for you."

The reporter returned to the newsroom and wrote an article based on the interview he'd completed: "As Murder Trial Looms, Granny Teaches Inmates to Knit, Pray."

When he finished, tears streamed down his cheeks. Dave's story, touching and engaging, made the national wire services. When Nick read his friend's article, he thought it might elevate Andrea to sainthood. It was that good.

Chapter 30
Monday morning
Bay County Courthouse

Andrea Pilinski's trial lasted four days. One day to seat a jury of twelve with alternates, one day for the prosecution to say she did it, one day for the defense to show she did it in pure self-defense, and one day for final arguments and jury instructions.

Describing the trial as speedy would be an understatement, but there were many reasons for it.

Judge Harold T. Kennedy had a reputation for overseeing a no-nonsense courtroom. He'd already declared his intention to retire well before the trial came on his horizon, and not feel any political heat—he wanted a smooth, clean trial that would survive appeal. He urged the prosecution and defense to stay focused and not get distracted by high-profile media coverage or the continuous presence of protesters.

The prosecutor was eager to get to trial. He had been feeling the heat all summer. The campaign to "Free Andrea" had not let up one iota since it was spawned at Dom Polski Hall with the help of cheerleaders, a marching band, and the passing of a donations basket. If anything, Andrea's notoriety had spread. Protesters marched for her daily at the jail, and they hounded elected officials during every public meeting. "Justice for Andrea" had gone from a rally cry to a demand. Skinner was chased by protesters wherever he went—even at home. The political pressure was immense, and Skinner was up for reelection. Nick begged the prosecutor for a private interview, but he declined, sticking with his insistence on short, infrequent news conferences to brief the throng of reporters. Questions during these scripted sessions were often ignored unless the answers would thrust the police or court into bouts of glowing praise.

Nevertheless, the prosecutor was confident because the evidence against Andrea was clear-cut, overwhelming, and undisputed. Authorities had Andrea's full confession to the shooting on videotape. They had the booby trap in Andrea's home, with fingerprints all over it.

Skinner even had the grandmother's four-poster bed brought into the courtroom. The holstered .45 caliber handgun was rigged to fire when a door was opened, just as it was in Pilinski's home. When the hammer on the .45 slapped the weapon's firing pin into an empty chamber, jurors gasped in unison. Nick could tell that the jury, fully attentive, was eating up the prosecutor's narrative as if it was spoon-fed candy. The prosecution's graphic demonstration was like dessert to the jury.

But that wasn't all. April Flowers and her grandson had admitted their roles in the shooting, receiving reduced sentences for full cooperation. They spilled all the details in court, including the number of other elderly widows in the South End that the grandson had helped with similar booby traps. One detail came out in trial that the *Blade* had not reported. Andrea had paid the grandson five hundred dollars for the weapon, which had a chiseled serial number. It had cost her two hundred fifty dollars for the booby trap rigging. Authorities were now pressing the younger Flowers about how and where he acquired the handguns.

At the end of the first day, it did not look good for the eighty-two-year-old. If she was convicted and sent to prison, Nick worried about the possible reaction from her growing legion of admirers. Would their protests become violent, or would they rise together and boot Skinner from office? Or both?

When it came time for the defense to stand up for Andrea, her high-priced attorney from Detroit did just that. Phillip J. Barkowski, animated and confident, presented a narrative about Andrea that made the South End woman seem like the personal grandmother of each of the jurors. She was the sweet, loving, adorable super-granny who made delicious homecooked meals and Christmas sweaters. He even recounted how Andrea baked Polish pastries in her kitchen with her grandchildren, which prompted warm smiles from the jurors. A tear trickled down the cheek of one man, who flicked it with a finger when he realized he was leaking.

Barkowski was a masterful speaker with a resonant baritone and a flair for the dramatic. He slapped the jury railing so hard that the judge admonished him—"That's enough of the theatrics, counselor," Kennedy intoned. "That's not going to fly in my courtroom."

A key moment came when Andrea took the stand in her own defense. The attorney guided her through her story from the moment she stepped into the confessional to the day she realized a confessed killer was stalking her. "When I understood she was after me, I was scared to death. She was a murderer, and she was tracking me. I had to defend myself. My friend gave me a solution, I took it."

Dave studied the jury closely as Andrea testified. He and Nick thought having her testify in her own defense might be risky. A flub or misstatement could be costly. But Dave thought she was calm and confident on the stand, truly believing she'd done the right thing. Barkowski had been cunning in prepping her to face the jury, which absorbed Andrea's every word.

Under cross-examination, Skinner lobbed softball questions to the elderly woman. He did not want the jury to see him manhandle America's Grandmother. He concluded his questioning by asking if her deceased husband, Ralph, had told her it was okay to set up a booby trap. It was a clumsy attempt to question her sanity in front of the jury.

Andrea kicked Skinner to the curb. "No, it wasn't necessary. I knew what I did was the right thing. I had to defend myself against an armed attacker."

Closing arguments were brief and to the point. The courtroom, overflowing for a fourth straight day, grew quiet as the lawyers prepared for their final moments in front of the jury.

Skinner's closing argument was that Andrea Pilinski knew exactly what she was doing when she set up the death trap for Natalie O'Brien. The killing was intentional, he said, and it was premeditated. "She could have called police, she could have left her home to visit a relative, she could have gone on vacation. But she didn't." The prosecutor paused for dramatic effect. "Instead she plotted to take Natalie O'Brien's life. The evidence is clear. You must bring back a verdict of guilty."

Barkowski reminded the jury of Andrea's angelic and pure nature. He reviewed Andrea's community work and good deeds via the Noon Optimists. Then he focused on Natalie O'Brien—a ruthless serial killer who snuck into Andrea's home with evil intentions.

"When this murderer approached Andrea's bedroom, she had two weapons and she planned to use them. Let me remind you of that. The killer carried a pillow in one hand and had a garrote coiled in her pocket. Natalie O'Brien was not going into that bedroom for a game of bridge or a friendly conversation, or tea and crumpets. No, she opened that bedroom door with the full intention of taking the life of this sweet grandmother. All Andrea did was defend herself by stopping her intruder in her tracks. It is every American's right to defend themselves and their homes. You must find Andrea not guilty."

Judge Kennedy gaveled the trial into recess. The jurors were escorted out, and the courtroom emptied. Nick chased Skinner into the hall to interview him. Dave cornered the smooth-talking

Barkowski in the Men's Room. Both men told the reporters they were confident they had made their cases with the jury.

Nick and Dave viewed it differently. The reporters' opinions were split. Nick was confident the jury would declare her guilty, though reluctantly. Dave had no doubt she would be found not guilty, and sleeping comfortably on Lincoln Avenue in no time at all.

When the judge reconvened, he gave the jury its final instructions. Kennedy took his time explaining the charges and law to the jury. He then reminded them not to discuss the trial or the evidence with anyone. He also warned them against listening to, viewing, or reading media or social media accounts of the trial. Fat chance of that happening, Nick thought. The jurors would have to be dead or comatose to not pick up clear and blaring vibes from both.

The jury were excused from the courtroom. Twelve strangers began the task of deciding Andrea Pilinski's fate.

Chapter 31
Thursday evening
Essexville

Nick Steele rolled into the parking lot of the Shot & Shell Bar on Woodside Avenue, looking for an old friend. He scanned the half-dozen parked vehicles and checked his watch. Andrea's jury had been out three days, and the reporter counted on his buddy to clue him into what was happening in the jury room.

It was shift change for Bay County sheriff's deputies. Nick hoped to catch Jimmy Thomlinson, a longtime deputy who wore many hats in the sheriff's department, stopping for a burger and a beer on his way home to Essexville. These days, Thomlinson had been assigned to the courts, and his current job was to guard the jury from Judge Kennedy's courtroom.

From the parking lot, Nick watched his rearview mirror as a black Jeep Wrangler pulled off the highway and stopped next to the bar's side door. Thomlinson stepped out, flicked a lit cigarette toward a butt can, and stepped into the bar. The reporter waited a few minutes, then hustled into the no-frills cement block building.

When he entered, the place went silent except for the juke box, which played a mournful country ballad by Waylon Jennings. It was so dark that even the shadows of the bar had shadows. Nick headed for the dim lights illuminating the liquor bottles behind the bar.

"What can I get you?" A bartender slid an empty shot glass in front of Nick.

"Peppermint schnapps and PBR wash," he said, his eyes adjusting to the dark. Only a handful of guys in the place. An elderly man and young woman were playing pool. Nick guessed it was his daughter. They both were southpaw shooters.

The bartender was tall and lanky and barely looked old enough to drink. "TRIXIE," in all caps, adorned her nametag. She poured a schnapps into the one-ounce glass in front of Nick, then drew him a half-shell of Pabst as a chaser. "Four bucks, let me know when you want another."

Nick tossed back the shot, swallowing in one gulp. He savored the wash. PBR was not his favorite, but it did the job. "Thanks, Trixie!"

Booths with bench seats ringed the walls of the tavern. Nick searched the room until his gaze rested on his old pal Jimmy, a cop with a big heart and a loose tongue. The deputy looked up from his burger just as Nick approached.

"Steele, not you, please no," he said, a grin chiseled into his square-jawed face. He looked out from his booth both ways. "Anybody sees me talking to you, and I'm dead meat."

"Hey, Jimmy. You're dead meat anyway." The two men shook and Nick took a seat next to him without an invitation. "I won't take much of your time, and then I'll get out of here. Got a question for you."

"I know why you showed up, and I can't talk about the jury room. The judge would have me skinned alive if he knew you was sittin' here," the deputy said, pulling half the onion off his burger.

Nick leaned in close. "Jimmy, I gotta find out what's going on in that jury room," he said. "It's been three days and nothing. We got a pool going in the newsroom. Most bets were on a one-day verdict, two at most. Are they locked?"

Thomlinson munched on his burger, chewing with his mouth closed. He did not pause to talk or put the bun back on the plate. Nick could tell he was thinking. Not the time to push, the reporter thought.

Nick raised his hand to get Trixie's attention, motioning for her to bring them a round.

"What's it worth to you?" the deputy asked Nick, pushing the last clump of burger into his mouth. He licked pickle juice and mustard from his hand. During his lifetime, Nick had only seen Dave mop up dripping condiments with his tongue. Jimmy was just as efficient. Impressive.

"Would a US Grant loosen your tongue?"

"Fifty bucks, are you kidding? I could lose my job," the deputy said. "Come on, you gotta do better."

"The only way I got the fifty was by stealing Tanya's lunch money." Nick hopped in his seat and held up his hands. "Reporters make less than cops. And teachers make less than reporters. This is about public service. Let me see what else I got. Might have another twenty."

As Nick dug through his pockets, Trixie delivered the drinks. Two shots, one whiskey and one schnapps, two PBR washes. Nick used the fifty to pay her.

"Ah, I guess that means I'm paying for the drinks," Jimmy said, reaching for the change that Trixie put on the table. "Can't tell you much. I only briefly go in the jury room and they usually clam up. But I do pick up bits and pieces standing outside the door, especially when it gets heated."

The reporter scooted across his seat to get closer to the deputy. He wanted to know how often the jury room became heated.

"More so each day," Thomlinson said, checking his surroundings. "They picked a jury foreman the first day and haven't been friendly since. They sound ornery, in fact."

"Have they taken a vote yet to see where everyone stands?" Nick asked. He knocked down his shot, winced when he felt the burn, and cooled it off with a splash of Pabst.

"On the first day, there was one holdout," Jimmy said in a low voice. "He flat-out told everyone he would never vote to convict. Said Andrea reminded him of his own grandmother, and he couldn't bear to send her to prison. Now a second juror, a woman, has joined him. They've dug in."

Nick asked if Judge Kennedy was aware of the deadlock. The deputy said Kennedy had received two notices of conflict from the foreman, and the judge had urged members to work through their differences.

"There's been some name-calling," the deputy said. "It's getting ugly. They know the holdouts are Polish—never thought I'd hear 'em use the P-word like that."

"P-word?"

"I'm not going to repeat it. Crude ethnic slur for Poles."

"Got it. That's nasty." Nick knew Skinner had wanted as few Poles on the jury as possible, fearful of exactly what Jimmy described. Among Poles and the Irish, ethnic loyalty could often trump the facts.

"Never knew the P-word could be used so many ways—noun, verb, adjective, adverb."

Nick shook his head warily. "Once that happens, it's hard to bounce back. Anything else? Do you think it's a hung jury?"

The deputy ordered another round from Trixie and paid it from the cash Nick had given him. They tossed back the shots and gave them a wash.

"I'd say so," Jimmy said. "The third Polish juror came out of deliberations crying after the last session. It's personal now. My guess is, she will join the holdouts and that will be the end of it."

Nick thanked Jimmy for the info, but he had one more question. He asked the deputy if he thought Skinner would bring new charges if this trial ended with a hung jury.

"Doubt it." Jimmy said, scooping up the change from their

drinks. "Word I hear is that Skinner doesn't have the grit. The pressure on him is way more than he wants. My money says Andrea goes back to being super-granny."

Nick thanked Jimmy again and suggested he leave a big tip for Trixie. "Be good to her. I'm a little thin on cash, as you know."

Chapter 32
Friday morning
Bay City Blade **newsroom**

Nick Steele had almost finished writing his hung-jury article for Friday's edition when he and Dave Balz received word from the courtroom that the jury in the Andrea Pilinski trial had completed deliberations.

Earlier the reporter had called other jailhouse and courtroom sources to confirm the information he'd received from Deputy Thomlinson. No doubt about it, they said, the jury was hopelessly deadlocked. The judge would declare a mistrial, and Andrea would be sent back to jail to await a possible new trial.

Nick had lots of quotations and background information from anonymous sources with which to build his story. Now all he needed was the official word from Judge Kennedy. They still had time to add fresh information for that day's newspaper, but they had to move fast. The managing editor would not hold up the pressrun.

As Nick and Dave hurried to the courthouse, another large crowd of Andrea supporters ringed the Bay County building as well as the jail. It was a festive atmosphere. Protesters marched and chanted. Vendors sold T-shirts and kielbasa and kraut. Children played in the streets, wearing "Free Andrea" T-shirts and singing "We Shall Overcome."

The reporters elbowed their way through the mob and squeezed into the back of Kennedy's court right before he gaveled the proceeding back into order. The boisterous noise and chatter disappeared as the somber and serious nature of the trial washed back in.

Judge Kennedy said the jury had notified him that members could not reach a unanimous verdict—though he had used the Allen charge twice to encourage one. He thanked jurors for their service and dismissed them, declaring the proceeding a mistrial.

The court erupted in wild celebration. The judge attempted to regain order, but it was hopeless. Word spread to the streets outside the courthouse and so did the celebrations. Andrea hugged her defense attorney as her relatives rushed to congratulate her. Dave hustled to interview her and her supporters.

Skinner and his assistants sat, mouths agape, staring at each other as the defeat settled in. The case wasn't supposed to go this way. They mumbled and cursed quietly and packed up their briefcases.

Nick pushed his way through the melee to catch the prosecutor before he left Kennedy's courtroom. "Will you file new charges against Andrea Pilinski?" Nick asked, almost shouting the question to be heard. "Will you try her again?"

"I must say I'm disappointed." Skinner stuffed papers into folders on the prosecutor's table. "I thought, and still believe, that the evidence was overwhelming. My office will review the case and decide how to proceed."

Nick didn't want him to slip away without a more definitive answer. "Is there a chance that Andrea will not face charges and will be freed?"

"Anything is possible," he said, pausing at the question in a way that hinted at the possibility of no new trial. "Like I said, we'll review and decide where to go from here."

Skinner broke away from Nick and fled the courtroom through a side door.

The reporters called the newsroom to top off Nick's story. Nick was disappointed at the verdict, believing justice had not been served. Dave was so delighted by the result, he could hardly contain himself. Regardless of the reporters' personal views, they were professionals and their duty was to report the news as evenhandedly as humanly possible.

On Lincoln Avenue, Andrea's neighbors gathered on her front lawn. They held hands and prayed, thanking the Lord for his good graces. While she was being held in jail, Andrea's neighbors and friends had kept up her home. They'd also cleaned the place from top to bottom after investigators finished processing the home for evidence. A visitor would never know that Natalie O'Brien's body had bled out at the end of the hallway.

Hazel Durant, Andrea's granddaughter and one of the chief architects of the "Justice for Andrea" campaign, shifted gears to "No New Trial for Andrea" mode. She worked her cell phone while taking part in Andrea's lawn party. Each speaker who had attended the kickoff rally at Dom Polski Hall last spring was put to work. She wanted the entire leadership of the Polish community to apply maximum pressure on Prosecutor Skinner.

"He needs Polish support to be reelected," she repeated to each official she called. "He needs our votes and our campaign contributions. Make sure he understands he will get neither if he decides to continue the persecution of Andrea Pilinski. He needs to cut her loose now. Enough is enough."

The leaders she called, still giddy from news of the hung jury, pledged unity and support. The Polish American Club and the Sons of Warsaw Association said they had a good candidate to oppose Skinner in the next election. She was a noted local attorney and a daughter of Polonia in good standing.

Hazel dispatched two teams of protesters, armed with "No New Trial for Andrea" signs, to march outside of Skinner's home around the clock. She would maintain demonstrations at the courthouse and county jail.

Andrea was almost free. Hazel and her lieutenants vowed to continue the fight to make it happen. They would not quit until the eighty-two-year-old grandmother was back at home for good.

Chapter 33
Friday evening
Kate O'Brien's home

Not everyone was ecstatic about Andrea Pilinski's hung jury. Kate O'Brien watched in stunned horror as the "Polish Princess" was celebrated as if she were America's favorite grandmother. The O'Briens, what was left of their family after the sudden deaths of Larry and Natalie, viewed her as a killer.

Kate was watching the Pilinski celebration spectacle on TV and cursing loudly, when the doorbell rang.

She pushed a curtain back to see who was at the front door. Nick Steele stood on her front step. "Oh no, not you again," she muttered. She released the curtain quickly, hoping he hadn't seen her steal a look. Should she ignore him and hope he went away?

Nope, she decided, he wasn't the type who just walked away. Kate waited a few moments. The doorbell rang again. She took a deep breath and yanked the door open. Before Nick could speak, she tried to head him off.

"Look, I don't have anything to say," she said, holding the storm door closed. "The last time I talked to you, it got me in a shitload of trouble."

"Yes, well, that may be, but I did what I promised you I'd do." He raised his voice to penetrate the storm door. "I told you I'd get Natalie's full story out there and that she would be treated fairly. Isn't that correct?"

She nodded. "You did. I was shocked. You were very fair to her," she said, relaxing her grip on the door. "What do you want now? By what they're saying on the news, it sounds like the trial is over."

Nick moved closer to the door so he would not have to shout.

"I'm here for your side of the story. Right now, all the focus is on Andrea Pilinski. But what's your view of what's happening?"

Kate did not respond. She retreated from the door, releasing the handle. Nick took that as an invitation. He opened the door and stepped into the home's entryway. The first thing he noticed were large photographs of Natalie hung in the living room and the kitchen.

Dinner was on the stove. His nose said it was spaghetti. A young girl, arms loaded with folded laundry, shot behind Kate, and Nick noticed that she glanced at him as she disappeared down a hallway.

"Is she yours?" he asked. "Definitely looks like you."

"Yes, that's Maureen. Morgan is helping her with laundry. Erin and Colleen are Natalie's girls. They're doing homework."

Kate led Nick to the kitchen, the same table where they'd talked during his last visit. "Want coffee? It's fresh."

Nick thanked her and sat down. She poured them both cups, then stirred the marinara sauce that bubbled lightly on the stove.

"I'm here to get your thoughts about the hung jury," he said, sipping the steamy brew. "Are you surprised by it?"

"In a town like Bay City—where we have more Poles than Warsaw—I'm not surprised." She sat down at the table. The hot coffee stung her lips. "That's an exaggeration, of course, but you get my drift. Her peers were never going to convict, regardless of the evidence.

"Andrea Pilinski got away with murder. She set up a device to kill my sister and it worked to perfection. And what are the consequences for Andrea? She spends a few months in the county slammer knitting booties with the other convicts, then gets to go home. How's that for punishment?"

Nick noted that Skinner still had the option to file new charges against Pilinski.

Kate laughed out loud. "Skinner is gutless. What a worm! You know as well as I do that it would be political suicide for him to go up against Poletown in the next election. It's not going to happen."

Nick suggested that Natalie's intentions were not pure when she entered the Pilinski home. "Don't you think her actions—she clearly went after the grandmother and she was armed—opened her up to the possibility of being shot? And what about the murders that Natalie and Larry committed? Their hands were not clean. They killed three men and set two more up to die. How do you justify that?"

Kate had thought this through. She said her sister had become disturbed after she was attacked and gang raped. She wasn't thinking right, Kate said. The assault really screwed with her mind.

"What she needed was therapy, not a .45 slug in her chest," Kate said, using her index finger to mark where the round had hit her sister. "She needed help. And I blame the priest."

Nick took notes furiously. "Natalie reached out to Father Bob and he gave her a bunch of mumbo-jumbo about forgiveness. He should have connected her with mental health experts. Instead he hid behind his vows and the Church and watched the whole thing play out. His hands are certainly not clean either."

Nick said Father Bob would have to live with what had happened and his own role in this case. He said the priest would face judgment later.

"Yeah, and everybody gets to go on their merry way except for Natalie," Kate said. "She's dead. She doesn't get a second chance or a do-over, like Pilinski and the priest. And what about her two children? Now they've lost both parents. I'm trying to be super-auntie, but young girls losing their mother in such a horrific way—that's tough on them."

As they spoke, Kate's oldest daughter, Morgan, came into the kitchen to test the sauce. "Hmm, yummy," she said. "Flavor really good, but the onions and celery are still a little crunchy."

Kate introduced Morgan to Nick. She remarked that she had read his byline in the newspaper. "How come you get to write about all the murder cases?"

"Just lucky," Nick replied.

"Homework finished?" Kate asked. The teenager scooted away without answering, which was an answer in itself.

"She's lovely," Nick said. "You must be very proud of her. How's her sister and cousins holding up under the pressure and media scrutiny of the trial?"

"They are okay. I've got them in counseling," Kate said. "They need to talk this all out, not hold anything in. That's what Natalie needed. She tried to carry too much and it made her an ugly person."

As he stood, Nick thanked Kate for being candid. They shook hands and he walked outside, waving as he swung himself into the Firebird.

After he left, Natalie called the girls to the dinner table. They pulled out plates and flatware. In minutes, dinner was ready.

The group took a seat at the table. Kate asked them to bow their heads to say grace. As was tradition, they clasped each other's hands.

Kate asked for God's blessings for her family. When she finished the traditional prayer, she ended with this: "And may God give us the strength and will to slay our enemies. We're O'Briens. When wronged, we always get even—and then some. Let us vow to each other that our souls shall not rest until we have wiped every Pilinski off the face of the earth. Amen!"

In unison, the girls declared, "Amen!"

THE END

Made in the USA
Middletown, DE
19 August 2023

36957118R00109